ROAD TO FREEDOM

Between Two Flags

An American Adventure

ROAD TO FREEDOM

LEE RODDY

BETHANY HOUSE PUBLISHERS
MINNEAPOLIS, MINNESOTA 55438

Road to Freedom
Copyright © 1999
Lee Roddy

Cover illustration by Chris Ellison
Cover design by the Lookout Design Group

Published by Bethany House Publishers
A Ministry of Bethany Fellowship International
11400 Hampshire Avenue South
Minneapolis, Minnesota 55438
www.bethanyhouse.com

Printed in the United States of America by
Bethany Press International, Minneapolis, Minnesota 55438

Library of Congress Cataloging-in-Publication Data

CIP data applied for

ISBN 0–7642–2028–4   CIP

To Mrs. Jo Knight
upon her retirement from
Eastside Christian School,
Fullerton, California

LEE RODDY is the award-winning and bestselling author of many books, television programs, and motion pictures, including *Grizzly Adams, Jesus,* and THE D. J. DILLION ADVENTURES SERIES, BHP's AN AMERICAN ADVENTURE, and THE LADD FAMILY SERIES with Focus on the Family. He and his wife make their home in California.

CONTENTS

PROLOGUE

From Gideon Tugwell's journal, October 14, 1933

I've kept a secret for nearly seventy years. It was something I had expected to take to my grave. But now, in my eighty-fifth year, it seems safe to reveal what an incredible experience was thrust upon me and others because of the Civil War.

There was Emily, the blond-haired Yankee girl who had been trapped in the Confederacy when the fighting started. She just wanted to return to her Northern home, but the war dealt her a huge surprise.

Nat, a runaway slave, had his own problems in pursuing a seemingly impossible dream against great odds and through many dangers.

I didn't expect anything unusual to happen to me on a hot July morning in 1862. However, that was before one of the most despicable men I've ever met rode his mule up the lane toward the house where we Tugwells lived.

TRIPLE TROUBLE

Gideon Tugwell felt his stomach twist when Barley Cobb turned his mule off the public road and headed up the dirt lane toward the Tugwells' small house. The boy had never liked the slave catcher, especially after he told Gideon he planned to marry his widowed mother.

With the family's two hounds baying at his mule's heels, Cobb approached the pigpen, where Gideon and John Fletcher had been examining a newly arrived black hog.

"Howdy, Gideon," Cobb said through his tobacco-stained beard. He dismounted, his hazel eyes darting to Fletcher. "Ye still here? I reckoned ye'd be long gone by now."

"These good folks took me in and nursed me back to health when the fever got me." Fletcher's words were so softly spoken that the boy almost missed their hard edge.

Fletcher added, "I'm trying to repay them in some small way by helping out until the crops are in this fall. Not that it's any of your business, Cobb."

"I'm a-makin' it muh business!" Cobb shouted. He angrily thrust his narrow face forward. "I aim to pertect this boy's widder mother from the likes of ye!"

"Mr. Cobb," Gideon said quickly while absently brushing the straw-colored hair away from his blue eyes, "Mama doesn't like people to yell."

"I ain't yellin'!" Cobb shouted. He shifted his eyes from the boy to Fletcher. "I'm a-warnin' ye flat-out, mister: I told them rangers I don't trust yore story 'bout losin' a hand at Manassas! I reckon yo're really a no-'count Yankee-lover, and I aim to prove it!"

Gideon exclaimed, "That's a terrible thing to say!" The raised voices made the hounds growl and bare their teeth at the visitor.

He shifted his weight to the left foot and drew back the right one with its heavy boot. "Call off yore dogs, less'n ye want me to kick the stuffin' outa them."

"Don't hurt my hounds!" Gideon cried.

"Ye a-gonna stop me, boy?"

Gideon hesitated, looking up at the scruffy man who stood nearly six feet tall and greatly outweighed him.

"He won't have to," Fletcher said in a voice as soft as a purring kitten.

Gideon turned to see smoldering fury in Fletcher's pale blue eyes. His face had suddenly turned dark as the summer thunderclouds already forming overhead. He set his feet firmly, his right hand curling into a fist.

Cobb sneered, "Ye talk mighty big fer a man with jist one hand, mister."

"That's all I need for the likes of you," Fletcher replied quietly.

Cobb blinked and dropped his eyes. His attitude instantly changed. "Reckon it wouldn't be fair of me to put ye in yore place, mister." Cobb turned and placed his left foot into the stirrup.

Gideon realized he had been holding his breath. He let it out in a relieved sigh.

From the relative safety of the saddle, Cobb glared down at Fletcher, and his warlike manner returned. "I done warned ye, mister." Cobb shifted his gaze to Gideon. "Up to now, I been good to ye 'cause I'm a-gonna be yore step-pappy."

"No!" Gideon cried. "Mama won't ever marry you!"

"I ain't told her yet," Cobb replied firmly, "but when I do, she will. Ain't nobody gonna stop me. So, boy, ye better mind yore steps real good. Otherwise, when I git the goods on this here Yankee-lover, them rangers might hang ye along with him! So make yore choice!"

★ ★

★ ★ ★ ★ ★

In the Confederate capital, Richmond, Virginia, Gideon's friend Emily Lodge joyfully lifted her hoopskirt and stepped over the threshold into Mrs. Lydia Stonum's parlor. She and Hannah Chandler looked up and smiled in greeting.

"I'm glad you're both home!" Emily exclaimed, removing her bonnet and shaking long blond curls to fall in ringlets behind her ears. "I just came from telling Brice good-bye at the hospital. He gave me a letter to give his sister in Illinois."

Returning to her childhood home in the North had been the desire of Emily's heart after her parents died and she had been taken into the Virginia home of her only living relatives. Her outspoken support of President Lincoln and antislavery views had caused her aunt Anna and cousin William Lodge to ask Emily to leave Briarstone Plantation. For almost a year, she had lived with the widowed Mrs. Stonum, waiting for passes that would allow passage through military lines into the North.

Mrs. Stonum shifted the sling that supported her right arm. She had broken it by tripping over a broom in a local hospital where she volunteered nursing wounded soldiers from both sides of the war.

Dressed in black widow's clothes, the forty-three-year-old woman wore her dark hair pulled back, as was the fashion. "How's Brice doing?" she asked.

"The surgeons say he's not going to lose his arm." Emily paused, her violet eyes showing sadness. "But now that he's better, they'll transfer him to prison until this terrible thing is over."

"At least he's going to live," Hannah Chandler said. She was an attractive twelve-year-old orphan with dark shoulder-length hair. Parted in the middle, it cascaded gracefully down both sides of her delicate face.

"Thank God for that," Emily replied. She frowned, then added, "I'm worried because Brice whispered to me that he plans to escape so he can fight again."

The widow assured her, "That's just talk from a young Union soldier trying to impress his girl."

★ ★

"I'm not his girl!" Emily protested but felt a warm flush touch her cheeks. He had twice said he was going to marry her when she grew up. She wasn't sure if he was joking.

Emily quickly changed the subject. "Mrs. Stonum, are you about ready to start on our trip?"

"Yes. An older woman from church will move into my room and look after this place until I return. Hannah and I found a roommate for her." Mrs. Stonum had married at sixteen and had three sons. They and her husband were killed in the war with the Union. "We've got our passes," she concluded, "so we can leave—"

She was interrupted by a knock on the door. "Emily, will you answer that?"

Emily glanced out the front window on her way to the door and recognized the four-wheeled town coach with its black body, distinctive gold stripe, and the Briarstone crest. A pair of matched bay horses stood in the shafts.

Bad memories swept over Emily, and silent alarms jangled in her mind. She braced herself, expecting to see her cousin William when she opened the front door. Instead, a gray-haired slave stood there wearing bright green livery with gold buttons on his swallowtail coat. "Uncle George!" she exclaimed, calling him by the affectionate title often given to older male slaves. Her eyes flashed to the empty coach. "What brings you to Richmond?"

Holding a black hat in his hands, he spoke in the common slave dialect. "Miss Em'ly, I nebber want to come heah," he began in a sad tone, "but young Massa William, his sista' an' de misst'es, dey send me—"

"I assumed that," Emily interrupted, anxious to know the answer to her question. "What's happened?"

"Dey say you read dis." He handed her a sealed envelope, adding, "Dey tell me wait fo' yo'all."

"Wait for me?" Emily cried in dismay.

George nodded, dropping his eyes as she took the envelope with hands that suddenly trembled. She tore it open while quickly introducing the old coachman who used to drive her around when

★ ★

she lived at Briarstone. Then he asked to be excused, saying he would wait in the coach.

Emily moved closer to the window to have better light, knowing the letter could only mean bad news.

Maybe Uncle Silas had been killed or wounded. Maybe something had happened to Aunt Anna, or even young Cousin Julie.

Emily scanned the letter, caught her breath, dropped heavily into a big chair, and closed her eyes.

"What's the matter?" Mrs. Stonum asked.

"My cousin William has been badly hurt in a fall from his horse. He, my aunt, and Julie want me to come help them until he's well."

"But you're going to Illinois!" Hannah exclaimed. "You finally got the passes and a chaperon."

"I know!" Emily said, her voice thick with anguish. "But I owe them so much for—"

"They've got nerve to ask that," Hannah interrupted in a huff. "How could they do that after William and his mother ordered you off the plantation?"

Mrs. Stonum put an arm around Emily's shoulders. "How long do they want you at Briarstone?"

"They don't say," Emily replied dully. "Here, read it for yourselves."

Mrs. Stonum took the note and skimmed it with Hannah looking over her shoulder. When they had finished, the widow handed it back to Emily.

"Both your aunt and William apologize for ordering you to leave last year," Mrs. Stonum observed. "They seem to really need you, and our passes are valid for sixty days. So if you want to go to Briarstone—"

"I can't go back!" Emily stormed. "Not after the way they ordered me to leave!"

"Julie wants you, too," Hannah said thoughtfully.

Emily softened as memories engulfed her. She and Julie had become friends. William dominated his sister the way their father had their mother before he formed a cavalry unit and rode off to war. William now also controlled the slaves. The family was strongly pro-Confederacy, and Emily stood for the Union. She had been vocally clear on that.

Hannah's voice interrupted Emily's recollections. "But if you do go back, you could see your friend Gideon. I saw the way he looked at you when he and that fellow Fletcher were here a week or so ago."

Gideon! A faint smile touched Emily's lips at the thought. William disliked Gideon, whom he considered "poor white trash" and whose family refused to sell him the small but rich river-bottom land adjoining Briarstone. Emily believed in Gideon's dream that someday he would leave the farm life he hated and become a writer in Richmond or maybe New York.

Mrs. Stonum said, "I know this is a terrible choice for you, Emily."

"I'm so mixed up!" Emily's voice almost broke as her emotions surged. "I don't want to go back to Briarstone! I've been hurt so much by the cruel things Aunt Anna and Cousin William said! But I owe them something for taking me in when I was left alone. Yet I want desperately to see Jessie!"

Emily's memory jumped again. After her parents died, she had been given a temporary home with her best girl friend, Jessie Barlow, and her mother. At Uncle Silas's invitation, Emily had moved to Virginia before Brice, Jessie's brother, joined the Union cavalry. He had always affectionately teased both his sister and Emily while they were growing up.

Emily took a deep breath and slowly let it out. "Why did this have to happen?" she asked, fighting feelings of both compassion and anger.

"Maybe you could go for a few weeks but leave for Illinois before your pass expires," Hannah suggested.

"That's possible," the widow agreed. "I could meet you at Briarstone, go north to the Potomac, cross the Long Bridge into Washington, then go on to Illinois."

"But what if William's not well enough by then?" Emily shook her head. "If he's not, and I stayed on, I might never get another pass. It took almost a year to finally get this, plus one for you."

"I wish I could tell you which is the right thing to do, Emily,"

★ ★

Mrs. Stonum said sympathetically, "but that's a decision only you can make."

"I know," Emily mused. "If I went to help, and my pass expired, I don't think I'd be welcome long-term at Briarstone. Yet I can't come back here because you have already done more for me than I could ever ask."

"Search your heart," Mrs. Stonum suggested. "What does it tell you?"

Emily was thoughtfully silent for a moment before musing, "I'm so mixed up I don't really know." She rose quickly. "I'm going to take a drive with Uncle George to think about this."

★　★　★　★　★

In a stand of trees bordering a dusty road south of Richmond, Nat's heart pounded as he cautiously raised his head from behind a fallen log. The fourteen-year-old had been a fugitive since his young master whipped him and he had run away from Briarstone nearly a year ago. He was weary from constantly watching over his shoulder for a slave catcher. But ten days into July 1862, he felt hopeful.

Lying on the ground, with only the top of his curly hair and dark eyes showing, Nat Travis ignored the sultry weather and peered at the road barely sixty feet away. Two rough-looking white drovers on horseback were walking twenty-four barefoot black prisoners south toward the North Carolina border.

The men, women, and children, bound with clinking chains, shuffled through the dust on both sides of a single, long coffle chain. Nat's gaze settled on his twelve-year-old brother shackled in the middle.

Until a few days ago, Nat had not seen Rufus for nearly two years. Their mother, two younger brothers, and a sister had been separated and sold after their first master died. Nat didn't know what had happened to the others after he was bought to be William Lodge's body slave. Nat had escaped on the Underground Railroad with Emily's help. Nat's very light skin, inherited from his white father, had allowed Nat to disguise himself in clothes that Mrs. Stonum had given him from her late husband's closet.

Nat had seen his brother but kept out of sight while following the slow-moving procession.

Licking dry lips, Nat swallowed hard, desperately trying to think of a way to rescue his brother. That seemed impossible, but Nat could not let his brother go south to an early death without trying to save him. Even if Nat somehow managed to free his brother, how could they escape in unfamiliar country?

A shadow fell across Nat, causing him to violently twist his head and start to leap up. It was too late. A white man with rivulets of perspiration coursing from under his wide planter's hat thrust the point of a cane against Nat's throat.

"Don't move, boy!" The man's gravelly voice was little more than a whisper, but it sent chills racing over Nat's body in spite of the muggy heat.

His captor added, "When I first saw you in those clothes, I thought you were white, but your curly hair gave you away. Why're you watching those slaves?"

When Nat didn't answer, his captor pushed lightly with the cane. "You want to join them or answer me?"

Nat dropped his eyes and spoke in the slave dialect, although he had been secretly educated and could speak proper English. "No, suh, Massa. I sho' don' want to do dat. No, suh."

Thinking quickly, he added, "My massa sent me to fetch him some wood fer de big house, but I seed dem on de chain an' had to look. So if yo'all'll 'cuse me—"

"That your master's house over there?" the man interrupted, pointing with his free hand.

Nat quickly glanced at the three-story red brick house standing on a knoll a quarter mile away. "Yes, suh. Sho' is."

"You're a liar, boy! *I* live there!" The man's voice hardened. "You're a runaway, so there'll be a reward for you. Get up and head for my house."

He used his free hand to reach inside his sweat-stained shirt and show the butt of a small pistol. "Don't even think about running, or it'll be the last thing you ever do!"

★ ★

THREE BIG
DECISIONS

After Cobb left, Gideon and Fletcher silently returned to the pigpen. Cobb's threats against Fletcher and himself upset Gideon, but not nearly as much as the possibility of the slave catcher marrying his mother.

She had told him that she, like most widows with dependent children, would have to remarry as the only way to support herself and family. Most eligible men were away fighting the Yankees, so Cobb was his mother's only suitor. Gideon didn't like the idea of any man replacing his father—especially Cobb.

Gideon and Fletcher stopped outside the pen and peered through the pole rails. The black hog stood in an opening that had been cut into a small shed as shelter from the July sun.

"Do Cobb's threats worry you, Gideon?" Fletcher asked, gripping the top rail with his right hand and resting his left wrist beside it.

"A little," he admitted, stepping up on the middle rail to peer over the top one.

"Cobb knows I'm no Yankee-lover," Fletcher replied, "but he's got his mind made up to make trouble. He's really mad at me, but the way he lashed out at you shows that he could cause problems for you or your family."

"But why you? You never did him any wrong."

"You really don't know?" Fletcher asked.

Gideon frowned. "I don't think so."

Fletcher abruptly changed the subject. "That hog is going to help feed your family through the winter."

Gideon realized that Fletcher wasn't going to tell him why Cobb disliked him, so Gideon studied the hog. "He looks mean," Gideon commented. "See how he's watching us with those little eyes? Notice how big his tusks are?"

"You'll only have him a few months, and then he'll be turned into bacon and ham this winter."

Gideon had begun to have second thoughts about having traded a heifer for the boar. "I know, but right now he gives me an uneasy feeling." He lifted one leg over the top rail.

Instantly, the boar squealed and charged across the small pen. Before Gideon could jerk his leg back, the boar leaped up. Wicked tusks ripped Gideon's pants leg.

He fell backward, but Fletcher caught him with his good hand and eased the boy to the ground outside the pen while the hog grunted and slashed at the wooden rails.

"Are you hurt?" Fletcher asked anxiously.

"I . . . I don't think so." Gideon quickly yanked up his torn pants leg. An angry red streak was already showing on his calf where the tusks had raked the skin, but there was no blood. "Thank God!"

"Better have your mother put something on that," Fletcher suggested.

"It's nothing. I'll be fine."

"It might be a good idea to at least let her look at that red mark. And better warn her and your brother and sisters to stay away from this pen."

"I'll do that." Still shaken by his experience, Gideon got to his feet and looked through the fence at the hog. "We had also better make sure that little Lilly can't open the door to this shed."

Gideon's five-year-old baby sister loved to explore the small world of the Tugwell hardscrabble farm.

"Can you walk by yourself?" Fletcher asked.

"Oh sure." Gideon turned toward the house.

"While you're doing that, I'll check that pen door."

"Thanks." Gideon started walking away when a thought hit him hard. He turned to look at the tall, strong figure striding

★ ★

around the corner of the pigpen. Suddenly Gideon realized why Cobb resented Fletcher.

★　★　★　★　★

By the time Emily had put on her bonnet, the initial shock of her relatives' request had been replaced by two deep but conflicting emotions: She was very angry and yet felt strong guilt. She walked outside while her heart and mind twisted and churned.

They made me feel unwelcome at Briarstone! she thought. *So I came to Richmond to get a pass to return to Illinois. It took almost a year to get that, and now that I'm ready to go, this happens! It's not fair!*

Emily choked back her resentment and tried to think rationally as the old reinsman opened the carriage door for her.

He regarded her with serious, dark eyes. "Yo'all goin' wit'out yo' bag, Miss Em'ly?"

"I haven't decided whether to return or not. For now, I just want you to drive me around while I think."

"Yes'm, Miss Em'ly."

"Oh, Uncle George, Nat told me that you can speak proper English, so you needn't pretend. But don't worry; your secret is safe with me."

"Very well, Miss Emily," he said with a faint smile. "Thank you."

"You're welcome. Now, tell me what you know of William's accident."

"Well, it was a week ago yesterday. Mistress sent me for the doctor, saying young Master William was thrown from his horse and hurt his back and ribs. Didn't break any bones, but he's sore and bruised. Has to stay in bed. Can't move without hurting."

"How long will it be before he recovers?"

"I heard Dr. Janssen tell Miss Julie that back injuries are hard to treat, and so he couldn't say how long young Master will be laid up."

I wonder if he'll be better before our passes expire, Emily thought. Aloud, she said, "I'm sorry to hear that, but why do they want me to come help?"

"I can't rightly say, Miss Emily. 'Course, you know your aunt is in poor health and takes to her bed a lot."

"I know about her 'spells,'" Emily admitted. She also knew that Aunt Anna never made decisions except about the household slaves, and Julie was quiet and submissive. Only William was strong-minded like his absent father, and now William was laid up.

"How is he managing the plantation?"

"The overseer comes to the house and gets his orders each morning. But I heard William telling his mother he's mighty unhappy with the way Mr. Toombs handles the slave driver and the field workers."

Emily had heard other planters talking about overseers. Most were poor whites and notoriously undependable. They moved on a lot, but Toombs had six children, so he had stayed at Briarstone awhile.

Emily thanked George and entered the coach. When she settled back, he shut the door and stiffly climbed up to the high, outside seat. Emily closed her eyes as the coach began to move. She tried to think logically.

Exactly why do Aunt Anna and William want me to come? They've got slaves to do everything, so why do they need me? It doesn't make sense. What am I overlooking?

She alternately fumed in angry resentment at her situation and then fought back intense feelings of guilt. After a while, she grudgingly admitted to herself that things didn't always go as planned. When that happened, the best had to be made of the new situation.

She opened her eyes and forced her emotions aside to squarely face the two choices.

I don't want to go back, she admitted, *even though that's the right thing. They're not only family, but I owe them a lot. On the other hand, there's no sense in getting into the same conflicts we had before I left. To avoid trouble, some things will have to change. Also, they'll have to agree I can leave before my pass expires.*

Emily began mentally making a list of conditions she consid-

★ ★

ered fair and should be agreed upon if she returned to Briarstone. She felt these would prevent a repeat of their previous conflicts.

I'll write them down as soon as I get to my room, she thought. *Then I'll have George take me to Briarstone to discuss them with Aunt Anna and William. He won't like them, yet in order for me to help, he might be agreeable. It's worth a try. But if it can't be worked out, then I could go on to Illinois with a clear conscience.*

A quiet peace replaced her resentment when she tapped on the coach roof to indicate that George should take her back to Mrs. Stonum's.

★ ★ ★ ★ ★

Under the prodding of the planter's cane and the threat of the pistol, Nat slowly rose to his feet. He glanced longingly at the coffle of slaves shuffling along barefoot on the hot, dusty road. All except his brother had their heads down, weighed not only with heavy chains but with the terrible realization that only death could free them.

As Nat started to turn away, Rufus glanced around and stopped dead still. His movement was so abrupt that Nat heard his brother's chains rattle.

He recognizes me! Nat realized. He wanted to wave to his brother but knew that would not be wise. He lingered a moment, his heart aching that his hope of helping Rufus escape had been thwarted.

But a slow smile spread across his younger brother's face. He did not lift his bound hand, but there was such joy in Rufus's face that Nat almost broke into tears. Then a drover leaned down from the saddle and slashed the boy across the face with his whip.

Fury erupted inside Nat so violently that he cried out at the drover's cruelty, but the planter's stout cane smashed hard against Nat's head, causing him to stagger.

"Stop looking at them unless you want to join them!" the planter growled as Nat spun to face him, bright anger in his eyes. The cane slashed down again, catching Nat across the mouth.

"You ever look at me like that again," his captor warned, pulling the pistol, "and it'll be the last time you ever look at anyone!

★ ★

Now, get moving! I'll get you home and find out who your master is. I need the reward."

Realizing the futility of resistance, Nat took one final anguished look at his brother. He had turned away and was moving south in the coffle. The sight stung Nat like an attack of angry hornets. Ignoring the slight bleeding from his lip, Nat lowered his gaze, but his heart did not submit.

He tried to send a silent message to his brother. *Don't lose hope, Rufus! Somehow, I'll help you be free!*

★ ★ ★ ★ ★

Gideon walked past his two little sisters making mud pies near the well curb. Their brother Ben was removing burrs from both hounds' fur.

Outside the back door of his home, Gideon frowned. His mother was silent. As long as he could remember, her voice was always lifted in song, usually a hymn. But he hadn't heard her sing since Papa died.

Gideon opened the door and saw his mother rocking in her chair. She had lifted her apron so it covered her face, a sure sign of something seriously wrong. Gideon instantly forgot about the hog's tusk mark.

"Mama! What's the matter?"

She stopped rocking and lowered the apron to dab at her eyes with a corner of it. She sniffed. "It's nothing; nothing at all."

"Your nose is all red," he replied, dropping to his knees beside her chair and looking into her bloodshot eyes. "That's a sure sign you've been crying."

"It's nothing to concern yourself with." She gave him a quick kiss on the cheek and stood up, letting the apron drop into place. "Forget it."

"I can't, Mama! Please! Tell me what's wrong."

She moved across the bare wooden floor to the kitchen table and picked up some eggs. "I was just going to make a cake for supper. What kind do you want?"

He followed her and slipped his arms around her neck. He had grown taller than his mother when he was only twelve, so now he looked down on her. "I've got to know."

Slowly she turned to face him. "I don't want you to take on my burdens."

"You take mine," he pointed out reasonably, "I'm old enough to help you with yours. So tell me."

She hesitated, her eyes misting so the light through the window made them sparkle like dew on a morning rose. "Your father would have been proud of you, Gideon. You're growing up to be such a wonderful young man."

"Thanks." He waited while she freed herself from his arms and again dabbed at her eyes with the apron.

"I don't expect you to understand," she said, her voice low and heavy with emotion. "But I'm . . . lonely."

"Lonely? But you've got Ben, Kate, Lilly, and me. You've got friends at church. Why should you—Oh." Suddenly it hit him. "Papa."

She nodded, new tears forming at the corners of her eyes. "Oh, Gideon! I miss him so much!"

"I miss him, too, but I guess not as much as you."

"Children are different from wives. Parents expect their young ones to grow up and move off on their own. But a husband and wife spend their lives together. They start out newly married with love that grows stronger year by year. They expect to grow old together and have their children come visit them with their own children. But your father didn't get to do that."

Gideon didn't know what to say. He silently reached out and pulled her back into his arms while fighting back his own tears.

His mother said in a hoarse whisper, "I can handle it fairly well during the day when I hear you children playing outside, and you and Mr. Fletcher working with the mule or building something, like that pigpen. But at night, when everyone else is asleep, I reach over in bed to touch your father as I've done for years. Only . . . only he's not there and never will be again!"

She started to sob as Gideon held her close, not knowing what else to do.

They stood in silent torment until she gently freed herself and whispered, "I'm sorry you saw me like this."

★ ★

"It's all right, Mama." He spoke in the same soothing way she had so often comforted him with.

But it wasn't really all right, he realized the moment he said it. Nothing would ever again be the same for her because Papa had gone to be with God, and only memories and a simple wooden grave marker were left of him. That and the loneliness; Mama's especially. But what could he possibly do that would make her feel like singing again?

Gideon thought about that when finally his mother said she was all right and sent him back outside. He walked toward the pigpen, where Fletcher was examining whatever he had done to secure the door of the hog's shed. Gideon had completely forgotten the hog's tusk mark on his calf.

He couldn't stand the thought of his mother crying. Somehow he would find a way to ease her loneliness so she would be happy again. That decision made, he strode toward Fletcher with new purpose in each step.

★ ★

HEADING INTO TROUBLE

Gideon enjoyed the Sabbath because it meant a break from the farm work, which he hated. Yet it was necessary to provide a bare living for his family. After church, while his mother prepared fried chicken, Gideon changed into old clothes and headed toward the barn. He carried paper and pencil as if he planned to make entries in his journal, but he really had another purpose in mind.

His heart beat a little faster as he prepared to take the first step toward making his mother happy again. Gideon didn't really want his mother to remarry because nobody could ever replace his father. However, he now knew how lonely she was.

Earlier she had told him that in order to survive financially, she had no choice. Barley Cobb was her only eligible suitor, and he would not stop trying to woo her as long as she was not married. Gideon shuddered at the prospects of the brutal slave catcher as his stepfather.

As expected, he found John Fletcher reading in the barn's shade, out of the hot summer sun. Nothing could ease the sticky summer humidity.

Gideon asked casually, "Did you enjoy church today?"

"Yes, except I wish the pastor didn't have to announce the names of members who were killed or wounded last week."

"There's a lot of sadness these days."

Fletcher motioned for the boy to sit on an upturned stump beside him. "I didn't know any of those people he mentioned, but I still ache for their families. I was also upset about his report of what that Union general is doing in the Shenandoah."

Gideon nodded, remembering that Fletcher had farmed there before joining the militia, and that General John Pope had issued harsh orders in the Shenandoah Valley.

Gideon asked, "Would he really destroy any house if someone fires on a Union soldier from that house?"

"I don't doubt it any more than I doubt that he'll have any civilian shot without regard to Civil Law if he thinks an act has been committed against his men."

Gideon didn't reply but took a deep breath before easing toward his secret goal. He said, "I'll bet you're glad to be living here where it's safe, even if you do sleep in our barn."

"I've never been treated better, Gideon. You, your mother, and the children have all been wonderful to me."

A faint smile tugged at Gideon's lips. *So far, so good!* "You don't have to leave this fall after the harvest is all done."

The former farmer turned his light blue eyes on the boy. "Yes, I do."

Gideon's hopes plummeted. "But why?"

"Because I gave my word to your mother that I'd only stay until then. That's to partially repay her for taking care of me after I arrived here and collapsed with fever."

Fletcher looked at his left wrist with the hand missing. His voice dropped, but his eyes hardened. "I can't serve in the army anymore, but I could still help make things hot for General Pope. This fall, I'll return and do whatever I can to drive out those Yankees."

"But you don't have anything left there!" Gideon's voice shot up in alarm and disappointment. "You said your family is all dead, and Yankees burned your place!"

Fletcher said very quietly, "Some friends and neighbors are still there. I love them, just as I love that valley. It's the most beautiful place I've ever seen. Or it was, until the Yankees invaded it. Right now General Stonewall Jackson is doing a great job against greater numbers, and I want to help, even if I can't do so as a soldier."

Gideon was so disappointed he didn't know what to say. His

★ ★

plan smashed, he stared in disbelief.

Fletcher took a short, quick breath and changed the subject. "Have you heard from your friend Emily since we saw her in Richmond?"

A vision of Emily Lodge flashed in Gideon's memory. He had been surprised nearly two weeks ago when he saw her for the first time since she left Briarstone about a year before. At thirteen, she was blond and pretty, something Gideon had not noticed when she lived down the road from the Tugwell farm.

"No," he told Fletcher, trying to ignore the strange new sensations Emily stirred in him. "But she should be ready to leave for her home in Illinois about now."

Gideon rose quickly, anxious to get away so he could think about what to do now. "I've got to do my writing," he said and entered the barn, his spirits sinking.

★　★　★　★　★

In spite of her apprehension about returning to Briarstone, Emily began to feel excited as the sun slid down the western sky that Sunday afternoon. When Uncle George guided the team around a curve and the last grove of trees fell behind, she caught her first glimpse of the plantation.

"There!" she exclaimed, leaning out of the carriage window and pointing to the stately three-story manor house surrounded by tobacco fields. "That's it!"

Emily leaned back so that Mrs. Stonum could have an unobstructed view of the house at the end of a long line of shady poplars.

"It's truly grand," the widow replied, her gaze sweeping the solid and square structure with the brick chimneys thrust toward the sky. "More grand than any we've seen on this trip."

"You'll soon hear the geese sounding the alarm," Emily said. She tried to avoid thinking of how Aunt Anna and Cousin William would react to what she had written down for herself as conditions for returning.

Emily pointed out the various buildings. "The kitchen is off to the right. You'll notice there's no covered walkway as we've

★　★

seen on other manor houses. That's because Uncle Silas had a tunnel built from the kitchen to the house."

"Oh yes. I remember you telling me that slaves going through the tunnel had to whistle to prove that they were not sneaking a bite of the owners' food."

She turned her head toward the tobacco plants. "It's very impressive, but where are the slaves? I thought they would be in the fields."

"They get the Sabbath off. Many of them tend their own gardens on this day. If you'll look off that way, you'll see a row of shacks lined up facing a dirt road but out of sight of the big house. Those are the slave quarters. Well, my relatives call them servants instead of slaves. I got myself in trouble for referring to them by the wrong word. Listen! Hear the geese honking?"

It was a strange feeling for Emily to experience excitement at returning while a knot of dread tightened around her heart. The coach turned into the long drive. On the front porch, Emily saw the Confederate flag flying from one of the stately white Corinthian columns. The door opened and a black woman stepped out.

"That's Flossie," Emily told Mrs. Stonum. "She's my aunt's personal maid. I'm sure she was sent to find out why the geese were acting up. Yes, there she goes back inside to report."

"Do you think she recognized you?"

"Oh yes. I could tell by the way she moved. Well, I guess we're about to find out whether I'm going to be welcomed or if you and I will go on our way to Illinois."

"Are you concerned?" the widow asked.

Emily frowned slightly before answering. "I have mixed feelings. I want very much to get home to see my friend Jessie and her mother. I'd rather tell them in person about Brice's wound and his being a prisoner of war. But on the other hand, I want to help Aunt Anna and Cousin William if it can be done without hard feelings."

Mrs. Stonum nodded and looked out the carriage window as it neared the big house. "That must be your cousin Julie."

Emily turned to look as a dark-haired girl ran out and stood between the columns. "Oh yes! She's grown since a year ago!"

★ ★

Sticking her head out the carriage window, Emily waved and smiled. Julie waved back.

The front door opened behind Julie, and a frail white woman stepped outside. Her black dress had a gathered bodice with long sleeves and pleated skirt that fell to within two inches of the floor. The style was popular in the South's humid climate. Her once dark hair was streaked with gray and pulled back to give her a stern look. Her thin mouth widened into a faint smile as she waved.

Waving and smiling back, Emily told Mrs. Stonum, "That's my aunt Anna. She doesn't look well."

"Maybe she's just concerned for her son."

"That could be," Emily agreed as the cold hand of dread again seized Emily. "I hope William's not worse!"

"We'll soon know," Mrs. Stonum answered as the carriage rolled to a stop.

★　★　★　★　★

On Sunday following his capture, Nat was awakened by a kick in the ribs. His eyes popped open to see the ceiling of the loft over the kitchen and a big slave, a teen named Orpheus, glaring down at him.

"Master and Mistress got to have their breakfast same as every day," Orpheus said. "You got kitchen duty with me. So get up before I help you the hard way."

Nat locked angry brown eyes onto the other's darker ones. For a few seconds, neither blinked nor looked away while each silently gauged the other's strength, and Nat quickly reviewed his situation and his plan.

Lucius Trumble, Nat's captor and the owner of a small plantation, had sent word to William Lodge to come claim his runaway slave. In the meantime, Trumble had turned Nat over to Orpheus to help him and the fat cook in the kitchen.

Nat inwardly raged because he could not help his brother. At every sunset, Rufus had been walked another twenty or so miles toward the Deep South. Unless Nat escaped soon, he might never catch up with the coffle holding his brother in chains. But there

★　★

was no sense antagonizing Orpheus, so Nat dropped his eyes.

"I'se up," he said, quickly rising from the corn-shuck pallet and lapsing into the slave dialect he had used since his capture. He had slept in the rough slave clothing the master insisted replace the white man's garments he had worn when apprehended.

"You can fool the master," Orpheus said in good English, "but not me because I'm also literate."

Nat protested, "I don' know what yo'all mean."

"Stop the act!" Orpheus aimed a kick at Nat's shins. Nat flinched as the heavy work shoes connected with bone. Anger flared in his eyes, but he caught himself and resisted the impulse to strike back.

Orpheus said triumphantly, "You talk in your sleep, so I know you can speak as well as I do."

Nat licked his lips, which had suddenly gone dry, but he did not reply. He waited.

"Also," Orpheus continued, "yesterday when I told you to get some molasses, you went right to the hogshead marked to show what it was. But there was an identical barrel right next to it labeled *Vinegar*. Yet you didn't ask me what was the right barrel, which also proves you can read."

Nat flinched but kept quiet, not knowing what would be best to do. He scolded himself because he had been so preoccupied that he had been careless. He would have to be more on his guard after this.

"Well?" Orpheus's harsh voice broke into Nat's musings. "You want a taste of the leather laid on your back? One word from me and the master will draw blood with every stroke."

Raising his eyes and looking boldly at the other boy, Nat declared, "I don't think you'll say anything. When an owner comes to claim a runaway, the reward might be less if that person isn't in top shape."

Orpheus took a quick breath as though he was going to disagree, but Nat's firm gaze made him shrug. "All right," he finally said, "but I know what you're planning, and it won't work."

"You can't read my mind, so don't try to bluff me."

"I'm not bluffing. My mistress not only taught me to read and write, in spite of the law and what her husband says, but she also taught me to think. From what you mumbled in your sleep about your brother, and what the master told me when he brought you here, I figured it out."

There was an air of confidence in Orpheus's voice that made Nat want to know more. "You think so?"

"I'm sure of it. You were watching your brother in a coffle when my master caught you. You think if you can escape from here before your master arrives, you can help save your brother. Well, it can't be done."

Nat knew it seemed like an impossible task, but that would not stop him from trying. "How do you know that?"

"I heard of a man who tried to rescue his wife from a coffle. They caught him and whipped him to death before her eyes. I also talked to some people who had been in a coffle. I learned there's only one time each day when there might be a very slight possibility of escaping. I mean *very* slight, but possible."

"When's that?"

Orpheus shook his head. "Oh no! I'm not telling you! Now, we'd better get downstairs and help the cook. She can be as mean as the master if she gets upset."

Nat followed Orpheus down the loft ladder, very aware that time was against him in three ways: He had to learn the weakness in a coffle, escape before William arrived, and catch up with Rufus before it was too late.

★ ★ ★ ★ ★

When George held the carriage door open, Emily stepped down just as her cousin Julie rushed up to give her a big, welcoming hug.

"Oh, Emily! I'm so glad to see you!"

"I'm glad to see you, too!" Emily cried, returning the hug. "You've grown!"

"Look who's talking!" Julie stepped back, shaking her dark curls in amazement. "You're now a young lady!"

Emily's violet eyes skipped past Julie to her mother. She still stood by the white pillars. Emily lowered her voice. "How are your mother and brother?"

"Mother is always complaining, although the doctor can't find anything wrong with her. But William is in pain, so he's quiet. Oh, I can't tell you how much it means to have you back!"

"I'm not officially 'back' until I discuss some things with your mother and brother."

Julie looked at Emily in sudden concern. "What sort of things?"

"Before I say anything, I have to know what's expected of me here." Emily turned to her traveling companion. "Forgive my manners, Mrs. Stonum. This is my cousin Julie. Julie, Mrs. Stonum, the lady who took me in while I was in Richmond."

Julie curtsied and welcomed the widow to Briarstone, then took Emily by the hand. "Come on, both of you!" Julie exclaimed. "Mrs. Stonum, come meet my mother, and then we'll go upstairs to see my brother."

Hurrying up the path marked by English box ivy, Emily prepared herself for what might become an awkward reunion.

CONFLICTS AND CHOICES

The chickens and livestock had been fed and the cow milked before the sun dipped toward the western horizon and Gideon finished writing in his journal. By the fading light in the haymow, he reviewed what he had written.

It seems so long ago that I saw Emily and Nat in Richmond. Maybe that's because life has been hard since then. Like when Barley Cobb threatened Mr. Fletcher, and Mama cried because she's so lonely. Then today Mr. Fletcher said he wants to go back to the Shenandoah and help fight against a Yankee general. It was terrible losing Papa, but it makes me feel sad to think of Mr. Fletcher leaving. I wish Mama could be happy again, and I wish I had someone to talk to about this.

Gideon stopped reading. He was tempted to write *someone like Emily*, but he wasn't sure he should do that. His thoughts were private. He didn't want to risk Ben or Kate finding his journal.

From a distance, he heard the back door open at the house and his mother calling, "Gideon! Wash up for supper."

He stuck his mouth close to a knothole in the back of the barn wall and shouted, "Coming!" He carefully hid his journal behind a loose two-by-four in the haymow and hurried toward the house.

★ ★ ★ ★ ★

Aunt Anna surprised Emily by greeting her warmly, then

★ ★

graciously welcomed Mrs. Stonum to Briarstone before leading them upstairs. Julie darted ahead and knocked at the door of her brother's bedchamber. At his invitation, she opened the door and stood aside for her mother, Emily, and the widow to enter.

William lay on a high, four-poster bed with a pale blue canopy. His face was drawn and his eyes clouded with pain. "Thanks for coming, Emily," he said weakly. "I trust you had a good trip?"

"Yes, thank you. Mrs. Stonum, may I present my cousin William Lodge? William, this is Mrs. Stonum. She consented to be my traveling companion from Richmond."

"Mrs. Stonum," William said cordially, "you are most welcome." His eyes moved to Emily. "You, too, of course."

She gave a small, relieved sigh. "Thank you, William." The secret fears that had troubled Emily since George brought the message about William's injury began to ease off. She hoped that William's civility meant he and his mother had really changed their attitudes. Emily asked about her uncle. He hadn't been heard from in months.

After a few moments, Aunt Anna suggested that Julie show Mrs. Stonum around the house and grounds. Emily saw the disappointment in Julie's eyes. She obviously hoped to hear more about what Emily wanted to discuss with her mother and brother, but that was to be private.

After Julie and Mrs. Stonum left, Aunt Anna sat in a Boston rocker by the fireplace. Emily seated herself on a small settee in front of an open window, but it offered no relief from the hot, humid July weather.

There was a short, awkward pause before Emily gently cleared her throat. "I hope you don't mind that Mrs. Stonum came here with me."

"Of course not," William replied. "This house has had hundreds of unannounced guests. With all those Yankee soldiers roaming around, it was wise to have her along."

"Thanks, but she won't stay long," Emily said. "Her plans are flexible, depending on what you expect of me."

A slight frown wrinkled William's face. "Flexible?"

"Yes." Emily quickly licked her lips. "I came to help if I can,

★ ★

and if we can agree on certain things."

"Such as?" William's voice was suddenly stronger.

"First I would rather hear what you have in mind for me to do here."

William glanced at his mother, who had very little to say when her son or husband were talking. His eyes flipped back to Emily. "Are you saying you might leave?"

"I'm just saying I don't want to have a repeat of the difficulties that arose last time I was here. We're family, and I want to avoid any misunderstandings or hard feelings. That's all."

"How do you plan to keep that from happening?" William's tone was edged with disapproval.

"As I said," she answered as quietly as possible, "I would rather hear your requests."

"Do you know how long it's been since anyone questioned what I say or do?" he demanded gruffly.

Emily quickly stood. "It seems I already have my answer. But I had to come find out for sure." She started toward the door.

"Where are you going?" William demanded.

"To Illinois." She stopped and faced him, forcing her tone to be calm but firm. "I came to help if I could, but that seems impossible, so I'm leaving!"

"Wait!" Aunt Anna's voice stopped Emily again.

Turning in surprise, she saw that her aunt had risen from her chair and held out an imploring hand. "Please, Emily! Don't go! Let's talk this over." She turned to her son. "Isn't that what you want, William?"

The wrinkles slowly disappeared from his brow. He nodded. "Yes, it is. Please, Emily. Sit down again."

She said doubtfully, "I don't know—"

"I'm sorry," he interrupted, his voice sincere. "Tell me what you want."

"I just want peace and harmony because we're family. Now, what do you want me to do for you?"

Her cousin again glanced at his mother, who nodded ever so slightly. William turned back to Emily. "All right, I'll tell you how

★ ★

you can help; then we'll hear what you have in mind. We'll work it out, so please sit down."

Emily thoughtfully searched the faces of both her aunt and cousin. She was still doubtful, but willing. "Thank you," she said and returned to her seat.

★　★　★　★　★

Gideon had just sat down at the supper table with his family and Fletcher when the hounds on the back porch suddenly bawled loudly and ran into the gathering dusk.

"Not again!" Gideon exclaimed, glancing hungrily at the platter of fried chicken his mother had just set in the middle of the kitchen table. "Mama, why does Cobb always come when it's suppertime?"

She stood up. "I'd be surprised if he dared return after the terrible threats he made against you and Mr. Fletcher. I'll go to the door. The rest of you eat before the food gets cold."

Gideon chewed rapidly on the meaty chicken breast while his eyes followed his mother to the front door. He heard her exclaim:

"Oh, Mrs. Yates! It's good to see you! Come in!"

Gideon sighed with relief as the editor and co-publisher of the village newspaper entered with a copy under her arm. Gideon liked the short, matronly woman with her blue eyes and determined-looking chin. She had offered him a weekly column to encourage his desire to become an author. He assumed the paper she carried was the latest edition with his piece in it.

Fletcher pushed back his chair and stood as Mrs. Yates followed Gideon's mother to the table. After greetings were exchanged and Mrs. Yates declined an invitation to join them at the meal, she sat in Mrs. Tugwell's old hickory rocker and held up the paper she had brought.

"I apologize for arriving during mealtime," she said, peering over the top of her wire-rimmed glasses, "but I wanted to leave a copy of the paper with Gideon's column in it. I also wrote a story about General John Pope." She looked at John Fletcher. "Since you're from the valley, I would like your opinion about Pope for the next issue."

★　★

Gideon remembered what Fletcher had told him about his plans for this fall, so Gideon put his chicken on the plate and waited for the answer.

"I doubt that anyone would be interested in what I think," Fletcher replied.

Mrs. Yates tapped the newspaper. "Have you read this week's edition?"

"No, I've been busy helping out around here, but I've heard something about what Pope has done."

"Do you know that he's holding citizens financially responsible for any partisan acts?" Mrs. Yates asked.

Ben leaned over and whispered to Gideon, "What's 'partisan' mean?"

"Guerrillas."

"Gorillas!" Ben's exclaimed. "Big monkeys?"

"Shh!" Gideon whispered, but everyone had already turned to look at him and Ben.

Mrs. Yates smiled. "No, Ben. This kind of guerrilla, or partisan, is a person who doesn't fight in usual ways. He's more independent and sneakier than regular military men. He makes many small attacks, sabotaging and harassing the enemy where they might not expect it. Have you heard of Turner Ashby?"

Ben shook his head, so Gideon said, "I have. He was General Stonewall Jackson's cavalry chief. He gave the Yankees lots of trouble as a partisan until he was killed last month."

"That's right," the newspaper publisher said.

Gideon added, "Cobb wanted to be a ranger, but they wouldn't accept him. He claims Mr. Fletcher is a Yankee spy, and he'll try to prove it so the rangers can hang him!"

"Gideon!" his mother exclaimed disapprovingly. "Please watch what you say!"

"It's all right, Martha," Mrs. Yates assured her. "I won't print that."

Gideon was sorry to hear the reproof in his mother's tone, but he was so angry at Cobb that words boiled out again. "He also threatened to have me hung!"

"Gideon, enough!" his mother cried.

★ ★

"Relax, Martha," Mrs. Yates said. "I won't print anything about that, either. But it was a despicable thing for Cobb to say." She looked at Fletcher. "Are you sure that you don't have any comments about Pope?"

"I'm not much of a talker, Mrs. Yates," he said.

Gideon, still angry over Cobb's remarks, blurted, "He's going back to the valley this fall to help fight against that Yankee general!"

"Mr. Fletcher, are you going to be a guerrilla?" Ben asked.

There was something in the man's eyes that made Gideon feel embarrassed for not controlling his tongue. His gaze shifted to his mother. She had a strange look that he had not seen before. It vanished in an instant.

Fletcher explained, "No, Ben. I'm just a man who's going back to help my friends and neighbors."

Mrs. Yates rose from the rocker. "I respect your right to privacy, Mr. Fletcher. Well, I have to go. I don't much care to drive by coal-oil lamps on my buggy, but I must stop by Briarstone to check out a rumor."

As Gideon's mother and Fletcher rose from their places, Mrs. Yates added, "One of the freedmen told me that he was driving by there earlier and saw a woman and a girl arriving. The girl looked like Emily Lodge."

"Emily?" Gideon repeated. "Can't be! When Mr. Fletcher and I saw her almost two weeks ago, she had received her passes and was ready to head for Illinois."

"I assume my informant was mistaken," Mrs. Yates said, "but I have to make sure, even if I'm not really welcome at Briarstone. Being in the newspaper business makes the Lodges tolerate me even if our views differ."

When his mother returned from seeing the newspaper editor out, Gideon's insides were churning with sudden concerns. "Mama, I know Emily should be on her way north by now, but if she came here instead, something must have gone terribly wrong. Do you suppose. . . ?"

"Now, Gideon, don't go worrying about her. It's highly unlikely that Emily came back here."

Gideon knew that, but he couldn't shake the feeling that maybe she had returned. Tomorrow he would find out.

★ ★ ★ ★ ★

Nat's mind wrestled with the problem of how to get Orpheus to tell him the one time that he claimed it might be possible to free a slave from a coffle chain. That had to be learned quickly, so Nat accepted Orpheus's invitation to attend a secret slave church meeting in hopes of getting the other youth to confide in him.

After dark, by ones and twos, some of Trumble's field hands and house servants slipped into the woods. It was a considerable walk because the meetings had to be far enough away that the master could not hear them.

After the 1831 bloody Virginia slave uprising led by the radical black preacher, Nat Turner, laws had been passed prohibiting slaves to preach. Most masters allowed their "servants" to sit in the back or in the hot balcony of a white church. Sermons were often based on self-serving quotations such as "servants, obey your masters," so Nat had not willingly attended such services. He didn't want to go now, but he felt obligated.

As they drew close to a clearing, Nat saw an older woman with her head in a large kettle. It was a common practice for slaves who wanted to shout aloud as part of their worship of God. Some masters objected to this, so a kettle or barrel was used to mute the sounds.

The dozen or so other slaves began singing and clapping rhythmically while Nat and Orpheus settled on the ground at the back of the open-air "hush-arbor."

Nat whispered to Orpheus, "It's been a long time since I heard anything like this. There's joy and excitement. I never saw this in the churches where my owners used to take us. It stirs something inside me . . . although I'm not really an emotional person."

"Listen to the words," Orpheus whispered back. "They sing of Moses telling Pharaoh to 'let my people go,' but they really mean themselves. Freedom for our people."

Freedom! The word echoed in Nat's mind with a deep, boom-

★ ★

ing sound. He knew the risk of being caught by patrollers, but freedom was worth it.

Freedom for Rufus and me—if I can reach him before he gets too far away.

Nat glanced at Orpheus, who was gazing at the North Star, barely visible above the treetops. It pointed to freedom, as men and women in bondage knew. For most of them, freedom was as remote as that star. Yet Nat had once successfully followed it to Canada but returned to search for his family. The star still silently called him, but he had to wait until Orpheus shared his secret of the coffle. *I've got to get to that soon, but how?*

★　★　★　★　★

The lamps had been lit in the big house when Emily descended the staircase into the parlor. Julie and Mrs. Stonum quickly rose from the settee.

"Well?" Julie asked breathlessly.

"Yes, Emily!" Mrs. Stonum exclaimed. "Are you staying, or do we head north toward Illinois?"

Emily hesitated a long moment before answering.

BUGLES IN THE
NIGHT

Emily broke into a smile and happily announced, "I'm staying—at least for a while!"

"Oh, I'm so glad!" Julie exclaimed, rushing over to hug her blond cousin. "I've missed you so much!"

"I've missed you, too," Emily replied.

Mrs. Stonum asked Emily, "You said you were staying 'for a while.' How long is that?"

"Well, our passes are good through September fifth—" She broke off her thought to ask, "Mrs. Stonum, did you explain to Julie about the passes?"

"Yes. I assumed that was all right with you."

"Of course," Emily replied. "As I was saying, even though our passes are good through September fifth, I want to leave a week before then in case the roads are clogged with military vehicles and soldiers."

A slight frown wrinkled Mrs. Stonum's face. "Does William expect to be back on his feet by then?"

"There's no way of saying for sure because you know how unpredictable back injuries are," Emily answered. "However, both he and Aunt Anna said that it would help them greatly if I stayed that long, so I agreed. They also said you're welcome as a guest until then."

"I appreciate their thoughtfulness," the widow said.

Julie urged, "Tell us what else you talked about upstairs."

"Well," Emily replied, walking to a fine mahogany Victorian

★ ★

love seat with the popular leaf design, "we agreed to be more tolerant of one another's views. I will try to watch what I say and they'll do the same, even if we don't agree on President Lincoln and abolition."

"I hope it works out," Julie said.

"Also," Emily added, "I can be friends with anyone I want. They can come here or I can go see them."

"Even Gideon?" Julie asked, sitting down beside Emily while Mrs. Stonum sat in a Queen Anne armchair.

Emily dropped her eyes. "Yes, even Gideon."

"That really surprises me," Julie admitted. "When you were here before, William wouldn't allow Gideon to speak to you. In fact, I never thought William would ever let Gideon set foot on this property again. I wonder why he changed his mind?"

"Maybe because I asked him," Emily suggested.

"Maybe, but you don't know my brother the way I do. I think he must have another reason."

Emily remembered when she had first met Gideon more than a year ago. William had threatened to beat up on Gideon just for speaking to her.

Julie explained to Mrs. Stonum, "There's always been bad blood between my father and brother and the Tugwells. When Gideon's father was alive, he refused to sell his farm, which Papa wanted very much. It's rich bottomland right next to our property. Now William wants it, but Gideon's mother and her stepson, Isham, won't sell."

"Gideon's family is poor," Emily admitted, "but he's going to be a writer someday. And even if he didn't have such plans, he'd still be my friend."

Mrs. Stonum prompted Emily, "You were going to tell us what they want you to do."

"It sounds easy," Emily replied. "Each day I'll relay William's instructions to the overseer and bring back field reports from him so that William can keep track of everything."

Julie shook her dark hair. "I was afraid of that. We talked about that before you came, and I was against it. You see, when William first got hurt, he had me take instructions to Toombs, but Toombs resented me. I don't want you to go through what I did."

"What happened?" Emily asked.

"It got so bad I couldn't do it anymore. So then William tried having Toombs report directly to him. That didn't work, either, because some of the other servants reported that Toombs didn't always tell the truth about what was being done in the fields. I know you'll tell the truth, and Mr. Toombs will get angry with you, too."

"I'm not going to give orders," Emily began, feeling a little uneasy about the arrangement. "I'll just relay messages. William will make that clear to Mr. Toombs."

Mrs. Stonum asked, "Are you to do any nursing for your family?"

"Not for William, but I will help Julie take care of her mother if needed."

Julie protested, "That's supposed to be Flossie's job, but she's such a scatterbrain!"

"I'm glad to help," Emily said. "All I ask is that we all make an effort to get along this—" She broke off her thought when someone knocked at the front door.

Julie glanced toward it. "Now, who would be calling this time of evening?"

They all turned to the hallway door, where Jason, the chief household servant, walked past in quiet dignity. A tall, slender, light-skinned man with curly gray hair, he wore a black suit and black scarf tie over white linen.

Moments later he reappeared at the hallway door and announced in good English, "Mrs. Clara Yates is calling."

"Mrs. Yates!" Emily cried, leaping up as memories swept over her. The newspaperwoman and her husband were widely suspected of being abolitionists, but only Emily knew for sure that they were. She hoped that no one at Briarstone ever learned of her part in helping Mr. Yates smuggle Nat and a slave girl named Sarah to freedom last summer.

"Emily!" Mrs. Yates exclaimed with a smile. "I heard that you were back! Lydia! I haven't seen you in years."

"It's been a long time, Clara," Mrs. Stonum replied.

★ ★

Emily explained, "I've been staying with Mrs. Stonum for almost a year. Thanks for suggesting I contact her when I got to Richmond."

"You must tell me all about it," Mrs. Yates replied. "But first, why are you here? Emily, I thought you would be in Illinois by now!"

"It's a long story," Emily explained.

"Come in and sit down," Julie said. "Mama's with William, but she'll be down shortly."

"Thank you," Mrs. Yates answered, following the two girls and the widow back to their seats. "Oh, I almost forgot! I just ran into some patrollers who told me they had chased a lone Union soldier on horseback. He got away from them in the river-bottom woods."

"A Yankee? Here?" Julie cried in alarm.

"So the patrollers claim," Mrs. Yates replied.

Julie glanced nervously toward the windows and the darkness outside. "Jason," she said, "run upstairs and tell Mama and William. They'll probably want all the doors and windows locked."

When Jason had gone, Mrs. Yates turned to Emily. "I want to hear all that's happened since I last saw you. And, Lydia, I want to know what brings you to Briarstone."

"All right. What do you want to know first?"

★　★　★　★　★

John Fletcher had retired to his quarters in the barn and all of Gideon's siblings were asleep when Mrs. Tugwell got up from her rocker. She looked across to where Gideon was writing at the kitchen table. "You'd better get to sleep," she said.

"I want to finish this story first."

"You need your rest. Go on to bed and I'll blow out the lamp."

Shrugging, Gideon laid his pencil across the paper. "Mama, I know you said that Mrs. Yates was probably mistaken about Emily being back, but I'm still concerned. Is it all right if I ride over there tomorrow and try to find out for sure?"

"Of course, but stay out of William's sight."

"I will." Feeling better, Gideon asked another question that

★　★

had been disturbing him. "Mama, do you want Mr. Fletcher to leave for the valley?"

She started taking down her hair from where she wore it pulled back in a bun. "Why do you ask?"

"If that Yankee general is as mean as Mrs. Yates said, and Mr. Fletcher goes there, he could get killed."

Her voice suddenly dropped to a whisper. "I know."

"He's a nice man; don't you think so?"

"Yes, very nice."

"Is there some way you ... uh ... we could keep him from leaving here?"

Coming around the end of the table, Gideon's mother sat down on the bench beside him and looked closely at him. "What're you thinking about?"

Gideon hesitated, looking into her tired eyes, which had been tinged with sadness ever since the funeral. "I've noticed you don't sing anymore like you used to do."

"Losing your father so suddenly took away all my happiness—except for having you, Ben, Kate, and Lilly. I know that all of you hurt, too. But we can't bring him back."

"I know. Nobody can ever replace Papa, and I wish you didn't have to remarry, but you said there was no choice. I mean, in order to survive, you said—"

"Wait!" she interrupted him, her eyes softening. "You think that if I have to remarry to support you and your brother and sisters, you'd rather have Mr. Fletcher as a stepfather than Barley Cobb?"

"I couldn't stand him, Mama! I'd run away or something if you married Cobb!"

She slipped her arm over his shoulders. "Don't say that! Sometimes life doesn't leave many choices, and we have to make the best of what comes along."

"But you have another choice besides Barley Cobb! You could marry Mr. Fletcher!"

She closed her eyes, and her mouth quivered as if she was fighting to control sudden deep emotions. "Gideon, you're old enough to know that a woman doesn't have the freedom a man does. A woman has to be asked. Mr. Fletcher hasn't done that, and I'm sure he's not going to."

"What makes you so sure?"

"Would he be talking about leaving if he was?"

The question stumped Gideon, but it made sense. Mr. Fletcher wouldn't be planning to go away, especially if he might get killed; not if he thought of marrying Gideon's mother. Silently Gideon slid off the bench, kissed his mother on the cheek, and went to bed.

He couldn't sleep. *There's got to be a way!* he told himself. *What I have to do is find it. But where do I begin?*

★ ★ ★ ★ ★

Nat lay awake in the hot, stuffy loft over the kitchen and kicked himself for having spent time with Orpheus and not even getting to talk about the secret of the coffle chain.

Orpheus grumbled out of the stifling darkness, "Why do you keep flouncing around and sighing like that?"

"I didn't realize I was."

"Well, you are, and I can't sleep."

"Sorry. I'll try to be quiet."

Even though the cooking fire in the great open fireplace below had been out for hours, the heat had been trapped in the loft. The two small windows at opposite ends of the tiny room did not offer any relief, letting in night sounds along with the oppressive humidity.

Suddenly, a bugle sounded in the distance. After the first few notes, Nat abruptly sat upright on his corn-shuck pallet to hear better. There was such a lonely, haunting, but strangely beautiful quality to it that Nat was greatly moved. He listened until the last notes faded into silence.

"What's that?" he whispered.

"It's something new the Yankees played a few nights before you came. I heard the master telling the mistress that he had heard about a Union general by the name of Daniel Butterfield who was so upset about the casualties at Richmond that he didn't think the usual playing of "Lights Out" was quite proper anymore.

"According to what my master said, the general kept hearing some musical notes in his head. He doesn't know anything about music, but he hummed it to one of his soldiers. He made the notes, and then the bugler was told to play it after "Tattoo" and instead of "Lights Out.""

"You mean we're hearing the Yankees clear across the James River?"

"Could be, but I noticed that one of the Confederate buglers played it back last night. I guess he liked it so much that . . . listen! There's another one!"

Nat quickly stood and hurried to the open window. He stuck his head out to hear better. The notes were the same but closer, obviously from one of the Confederate encampments on the west side of the James. Again, the same notes lingered in the night air and slowly died out. "How come I didn't hear it before?" Nat asked.

"Because you've been so preoccupied with your own thoughts. Listen! There's another one starting."

Farther away, a third bugler repeated the simple but unfamiliar melody. There was a quality of finality in the sad notes that seemed to reach inside Nat's heart. At the same time, he sensed hope in the music.

It's so touching that both North and South are playing the same melody. I wonder what it's called? he thought to himself as he slowly returned to his pallet.

"Oh, Nat," Orpheus said in the darkness, "I don't want to spoil the mood, but have you given any more thought to what I said about a coffle chain?"

Nat realized that the other youth wanted to torment him, but he would not admit how desperately he longed to know the chain's secret. "I've got other things on my mind," he said, "so good night."

Orpheus chuckled but fell silent.

In spite of his best efforts not to think about it, Nat's thoughts went to his brother. He was now miles away and getting farther every day. Nat could have tried running away to follow Rufus, but what good would that do if there was no way to free him from his chains?

Suddenly Nat thought of a possibility. He asked, "Is this plantation self-sufficient?"

"What kind of a crazy question is that?"

"Is it?" Nat persisted. "The one where I was before I ran away had everything: smokehouse, tobacco barns, even a blacksmith."

"We got all that and more. Now, if I hear another word out of you tonight, I'm going to pitch you headfirst out of that window!"

"Not another word," Nat whispered. *A blacksmith would know about chains. Now if I can just get away from the kitchen long enough to talk to him . . .*

Nat slept and dreamed that all the slaves at the church meeting were free. So were he and Rufus. But some white folks rushed up with whips and chains, and Nat was again a slave, yet Rufus was still free.

Nat awakened, but the images were so vivid that gooseflesh erupted on his arms. He rubbed them slowly, and although the bumps subsided, the fear remained.

THE INTRUDER

At dawn, Gideon and Fletcher started the daily chores in the barn. Fletcher climbed into the haymow with a pitchfork while Gideon absently milked the cow. He knew he could never go off to the big city to write his books unless his mother was happily remarried to someone who could run the farm. Fletcher could do that well, but he had not shown any interest in Martha Tugwell. In the fall, Fletcher planned to move on.

Isham, Gideon's older half brother, perhaps would return to farming after the war. But he could also be killed or wounded so badly that he would not be able to handle farm life. That left Barley Cobb as the only eligible man, and Gideon was dead set against having him as a stepfather. Gideon told himself, *I've got to find a way to get Mama and Mr. Fletcher together—somehow.*

"Gideon, you about finished?" Fletcher asked.

"Huh? Oh yes. I'm finished." He glanced down at the bucket between his legs and frowned. He rose, picked up his three-legged stool, and carried it with the pail to where Fletcher had finished feeding Hercules, the mule.

"Look at this," Gideon said. "I've stripped her, but the pail isn't full."

Fletcher glanced into the foaming whiteness. "That's down from her usual amount, but not by much."

"But why would she be down at all?" Gideon turned to look back at the cow. "I sure hope she's not going dry."

"It's probably nothing important," Fletcher said as he and

Gideon started across the open dirt area toward the small house. The old red rooster flew up on top of the chicken coop, flapped his wings, and crowed.

"I love that sound. I hate farming, but I love the sounds. I love the dawn sounds best. It's—"

Gideon stopped abruptly and stared at the chicken pen. "How did that gate get open? I shut it tight last night."

"I'll close it," Fletcher volunteered, turning aside and striding with long legs toward the pen.

Gideon set the pail down and watched as the gate swung shut and the piece of wood on a nail was turned to secure it. Gideon felt good having Fletcher around.

"Hey, Gideon. Take a look at this."

The concern in Fletcher's voice prompted the boy to pick up the bucket of milk and hurry forward. As he neared, Fletcher pointed to some tracks in the dust.

"What do you make of these?" he asked.

Gideon bent to look closer. "Boot prints, but not mine or Ben's."

"Nor mine," Fletcher said.

"They weren't there last evening," Gideon said thoughtfully. "Mama had me check for eggs just before dark. So somebody was here during the night—Cobb!"

"I suppose he could have been," Fletcher admitted.

"Had to be!" Gideon said emphatically. "He sneaked around to try to find something against you—and maybe me."

Fletcher glanced toward the smokehouse. "Look! That door's open, too!"

They hurried toward the small wooden structure with the good smell of woodsmoke. Fletcher opened the door wider. The interior was dark, but there was enough light from outside to show the hams and slabs of bacon hanging from ceiling poles.

"One's missing!" Gideon exclaimed, pointing. "Last night I moved a side of bacon from the overhead to this peg closest to the door. That Cobb!" Gideon's voice rose in anger. "He's the most low-down person I ever met!"

Fletcher stooped to check for footprints outside the door.

★ ★

"Same tracks here. They lead off toward the swamp."

"Cobb probably hid his mule down there, then slipped in while we were asleep. But why didn't the dogs bark?"

"Either they recognized him, or he was very quiet."

"They always bark when he shows up," Gideon said.

Fletcher removed his black slouch hat and scratched his head. "Then maybe it wasn't Cobb."

"Who else could it have been?"

"I don't know. Maybe someone really desperate and hungry. He might look for eggs to go with his bacon, and possibly milk the cow for enough to round out his meal."

"Nobody could do that without arousing the hounds."

"Maybe they were off hunting in the swamp by themselves."

"But I didn't hear them baying," Gideon said.

"Neither did I," Fletcher added. "But if they didn't strike a trail, they wouldn't have sounded off. Anyway, after breakfast, I'll try to follow these footprints."

"I'll go with you."

"Thanks, but that's not necessary."

"All right," Gideon said with relief, recalling that he planned to ride by Briarstone to see if Emily was back, as Mrs. Yates thought. His anger at Cobb was replaced by concern for why Emily would have returned.

★　★　★　★　★

Emily heard the cow's horn sounding from the slave quarters before dawn. She quietly slid out of the high bed, dressed by lamplight, and slipped out of the big house with her cousin William's instructions clearly in mind. Julie had volunteered to go with her to see Lewis Toombs, but Emily had discouraged that.

She found the stocky forty-year-old white overseer just as a young slave boy handed him the reins prior to swinging into the saddle.

"Mr. Toombs," she called, hurrying toward him. "One moment, please."

He turned to look at her from under a wide planter's hat. His unshaven jaw seemed to clench at the sight of the blond girl in a hoopskirt, which she held off the ground with both hands. She had not had time to put up her hair, so it cascaded in golden ripples down over her shoulders.

"My cousin William sent me," she said quickly, gazing into hard brown eyes and a face burned brown and furrowed by the sun. "I'm Emily Lodge."

"Miss Emily," he said uncertainly, bobbing his head.

There was a hardness about his eyes that unnerved Emily. She said, "I lived here last year. Silas Lodge is my uncle."

"I remember my oldest boy telling me about you. I'll say one thing for him: He was right about you being the prettiest little filly in these parts."

Taken aback, Emily murmured, "Thank you." She quickly regained control of herself. "William asked me to help until he's able to return to the fields himself."

She saw his black eyebrows drop like vultures settling over a carcass. He asked, "You replacing his little sister?"

"I've brought today's instructions from William," she replied, ignoring his question. "He wants you to—"

"I don't take orders from females," Toombs broke in, "especially Yankees. I can run this place by myself until William is well enough to ride again."

Emily ignored the "Yankee" slur; Julie's report on her experience with the overseer kept Emily from being taken totally by surprise at Toombs' attitude. She said, "I'm just trying to help—"

"I don't need your help, miss!" He settled into the saddle. "If William doesn't like it, he can come do this work himself!"

Emily grabbed the horse's bridle. "You know he can't do that! It'll be some time before—"

"That's not my problem! Now, let go and step back."

"Not yet!" Emily's voice hardened with resolve. She gazed steadily up into the man's face. "I was sent here to give you William's instructions. When I've done that, then I'll release your horse—not before."

Toombs' heavy eyebrows shot up so that even the whites of his eyes showed. He lifted his booted heels as if to spur the horse. "Get out of my way, miss!"

★ ★

Emily held her ground. "I will when you've heard the instructions I've brought you."

He reached for the small leather whip looped around the saddle horn. "I'm tired of talking about this!"

"You wouldn't dare!"

He glared at her, teeth clenched, eyes afire with fury, but the girl did not move. Slowly he nodded. "All right, I'll listen, but this is the last time!"

"Perhaps it is," she replied evenly, her voice calm but firm. "I would rather not have this responsibility, but since I do, I would appreciate your making it as easy as possible for both of us."

She slowly released the bridle but did not step back, suspecting Toombs would otherwise kick the horse and shoot past her. "Thank you, Mr. Toombs. Now, here's what William asked me to tell you."

She relayed half a dozen instructions, taking care to keep her tone level and firm. When she had finished, she looked up and asked, "Do you have any questions?"

For a few heartbeats, he did not answer. Then he nodded. "Just one. How long are you going to do this?"

"No longer than the end of August, God willing. Then I'm off to Illinois."

Toombs made a grunting sound. "I see."

With a disarming smile, she took two steps backward. "I think we can work together that long, don't you?"

He didn't answer but loosened the reins, clucked to the horse, and slowly rode away. She heard a slight chuckle behind her and turned quickly. The boy who had held the reins for the overseer spun away, but not before Emily saw a wide grin on his face.

She looked beyond him and saw two other dark faces smiling in glee. None of them spoke, but Emily heard stifled laughter as they hurried away.

Well, she admitted to herself, *at least somebody enjoyed this. I wish I had. But it's only a half dozen or so weeks.*

Her thoughts jumped as she started walking back toward the house. *I've got to let Gideon know I'm back.*

She stopped abruptly as an idea flashed across her mind. For

★ ★

a moment, she stood still while the notion quickly settled into a clear form. She smiled to herself.

Of course! Why didn't I think of that before? Then she shook her head. *William's not going to like it*, she realized, *but now's as good a time as any to see if he meant what he said*. She hurried toward the house, anxious to put her plan into action.

★　★　★　★　★

It took Nat until midmorning to figure out how to be sent on an errand to the blacksmith without arousing suspicion about his motives. He risked a hard cuffing from the fat cook, who had absolute power in the kitchen.

While carrying a heavy basket of fresh vegetables across the uneven floor stones, Nat pretended to stumble. He threw up both hands and struck two old-fashioned oil lamps suspended by long metal rods from the high ceiling.

The lamps were not as practical as the new kerosene lights, but Cook liked the two ornamental roosters with long, curving tails that graced the top of the flat lamps. She whirled around as Nat fell with the lamps clattering to the floor. One rooster survived the fall, but the other instantly lost his beautiful tail.

The cook, perspiration pouring off the fat folds in her neck, spun from the open hearth with surprising agility for such a large woman. The heavy metal ladle in her hand fell in rapid strokes around Nat's head and shoulders. She emphasized them with strong words while Nat protected himself as best he could.

When the cook began to wheeze from shortness of breath, she stopped to rest. Nat bent to pick up the broken rooster in one hand and its tail in the other.

"I'se gwine fix dis fo' yo'll," he said, using the slave dialect to continue hiding his literacy from all except Orpheus. "'Smith kin fix dis, sho' 'nuf."

"Den fix it!" the cook roared, hoisting the ladle again. "Git outa heah!"

Nat backed out, bowing and acting as humble as possible, aware that Orpheus was watching him with narrowed eyes. Nat didn't care. He scampered toward the blacksmith shop.

★　★

The smithy was a big, sullen man with a pockmarked face and biceps that seemed as big around as a washtub. He didn't speak but merely grunted and nodded when Nat showed him the broken rooster parts.

"I'se gwine wait," Nat said, backing up from the heat of the glowing red coals. He looked around at the broken tools and pieces of machinery waiting to be repaired. He found what he had expected: several lengths of heavy chain hanging from the wall.

"Dis heah," he said, touching a long chain so it rattled loudly enough to be heard above the puffing of the hand-held leather bellows. "Dis cof'l?"

The smithy lowered the bellows and picked up a horseshoe with a pair of long-handled metal tongs. "Naw," he said, shoving the horseshoe into the glowing coals.

"Yo'all been in dem cof'ls?" Nat asked, hoping to draw the un-communicative slave into a conversation.

The smithy lifted his free hand with the huge biceps and wiped great drops of perspiration from his brow. "Leab dis," he growled, motioning with his chin toward the broken rooster.

"De cook, she done tol' me . . ." Nat lied, but the smithy thrust his pockmarked face forward on a neck as thick as a wagon axle. Quickly Nat nodded. "Yes'suh. Leab dis heah," he said and walked outside.

There he stopped and sighed. *It was a good idea*, he told himself, *but it didn't work. I guess I'll have to go back to working on Orpheus.*

But as Nat hurried back to the kitchen, he had a hard time keeping up his spirits. His brother was getting farther and farther away, and Nat still didn't have the slightest idea of what weakness a coffle chain had.

★　★　★　★　★

The sun had climbed halfway up into the scorching July sky before Gideon slid off of Hercules' bare back in the last clump of river-bottom trees on the Tugwell land. He carried a hammer in his hand as if he were going to make some repairs in the snake

★　★

fence that marked the end of his family's property and the start of Briarstone Plantation.

There, field hands were working a good half a mile away, unmindful of anything except making their quota so they could escape the overseer's wrath or the black slave driver's punishing blows. The overseer on his horse had his back turned, so Gideon breathed a little easier.

He walked along the fence as if looking for rails to be repaired, but his eyes were on the big house. There was no sign of Emily or Julie.

I have to get closer, he thought, feeling a little safer because William was confined to his bedchamber, which was on the other side of the house. Still, Gideon's heart sped up as he recalled the many beatings that the older, heavier William had given him over the years.

Gideon circled back toward the clump of trees where he had tied his mule. By staying in the shelter of the trees, Gideon was within a couple hundred yards of the house when he glimpsed movement at a second-story window. It opened, and a blond head showed as the shutters were pushed back.

"Emily!" he exclaimed aloud. "She *is* back!"

He whipped off his hat, but she pulled back into the room before he could swing it around his head in hopes of attracting her attention.

I've got to see her, no matter what William says! He turned toward his mule and blinked in surprise.

"Hey!" he yelled at the sight of a young man untying Hercules. "Hey! Stop! That's my mule!"

DREAMS OF FREEDOM

Emily finished putting her few belongings into the armoire of the second-story bedchamber while Julie sat on the high bed and disapprovingly shook her dark hair.

"William's not going to like it," she warned, "so what're you going to do if he says you can't?"

"I've been thinking about that. I wish he would finish bathing so I can talk to him."

"His new body servant is so slow!" Julie exclaimed. "Nat was the best one William ever had."

A twinge of guilt made Emily keep her face hidden behind the open armoire door. She loved Julie very much, but Emily could not even tell her about the role she and the Yateses had played in helping Nat escape to freedom.

"Since he's not back," Emily said, closing the armoire door, "I suppose that means he was never caught."

"No, even though William offered a good reward."

Feeling relieved, and keeping her back to Julie, Emily walked to the window she had opened moments ago.

Julie added, "He's probably in Canada by now."

"I suppose." Emily saw movement beyond the snake fence that marked the end of Briarstone property and the start of the Tugwells'. Someone on foot ran out of the woods, chasing after a mule with a rider entering a clearing. Emily blinked and looked closer.

"Julie! Come here!" she called over her shoulder.

"What is it?" Julie asked, coming up beside her.

★ ★

"Look beyond the fence. See them?"

"That's just Gideon Tugwell playing with his little brother on the mule."

"I don't think so!" Emily cried. "That rider's too tall to be his brother."

"You're right. That's a man riding. But why're they running so hard?"

"I think he's stealing Gideon's mule!"

"Well, if he is, Gideon's never going to catch him; not on foot. See? The rider is pulling away!"

Emily nodded as Gideon stopped running, whipped off his hat, and threw it down hard in front of him in obvious frustration. "Come on, Julie! Let's go down there!"

"You can't help him!" she protested. "Besides, William will be ready to see you in a few minutes."

Emily didn't answer but dashed downstairs.

★　★　★　★　★

Gideon helplessly watched Hercules and the rider who had stolen him disappear into another grove of trees. Gideon sank dejectedly onto the warm earth of the river bottom. Losing the family's only mule was a major blow to a small dirt farm. Without Hercules, there would be no plowing, no hauling, and no trips to church on Sunday.

Gideon thought of trying to track the mule, but that was probably useless. His thoughts jumped. The rider had been a stranger not much older than Gideon. Maybe Barley Cobb had arranged for Hercules to be stolen so that even more financial pressure would be placed upon Gideon's mother. The thought infuriated Gideon, and he forced himself to his feet.

I may as well go tell Mama and Fletcher, he thought with a heavy sigh.

His back was to the rail fence as he started toward his small house. A voice hailed him. He whirled around and stared in disbelief at Emily and Julie.

"Emily!" he cried, breaking into a run toward them, "I heard you might be back!"

★　★

"Hello, Gideon," she said, smiling warmly and tossing her long blond tresses in a way that made them shimmer like polished gold in the sunlight.

Gideon nodded and said hello to Julie; then he quickly swung back to Emily and returned her smile. "Why aren't you in Illinois?"

"It's taken me almost a year to get a pass through the military lines," she replied, her face sobering. "I finally got it, but then her brother got hurt." She nodded toward Julie before explaining, "I'm here to help out."

"I was sorry to hear about William's accident," Gideon replied, glancing at Julie. "Is he any better?"

"He's recovering slowly but surely," she replied.

Gideon's eyes snapped back to Emily. He was so glad to see her that he felt he would burst with happiness, but suddenly he felt a little awkward and dropped his gaze. "How long will you be here?"

"My pass expires September fifth, but I want to leave a week early so I don't get caught in some battle before my traveling companion and I reach the Potomac."

Gideon's insides twisted into a knot. "So soon?"

Sadness tinged Emily's reply. "I'm afraid so."

Julie asked, "What happened to your mule?"

"Stolen!" Gideon said bitterly. "Happened while I was only a short distance away!"

"Did you recognize the thief?" Julie asked.

"Never saw him before. I think he was wearing part of a Yankee uniform, but I'm not sure."

"Could be a deserter," Julie guessed. "My brother says the patrollers have reported seeing some slipping around, but they haven't caught anyone so far."

"You'd better let the sheriff know," Emily said.

Gideon shook his head. "The regular sheriff went off to fight the Yankees when Jeff Davis started drafting men between eighteen and thirty-five back in April. Only one old deputy is left."

There was no use in telling the girls how much more desperate it made his mother's situation. "But we'll get by." The

★ ★

awkward feeling swept over him again. He wanted to tell her how glad he was to have her back, even for a while. Instead, he said, "I'd better get back to the house and let my mother know what happened."

Emily quickly asked, "Are you still writing?"

"I'm trying," he admitted.

"With the schools closed this past year, who's been teaching you reading and spelling?"

"Mrs. Yates helps some, but I need a lot more."

Emily hesitated, then asked, "Would you like me to help you?"

"Would I?" His face lit up with joy, then instantly fell. "But that won't work. You know William told me I couldn't even speak to you. If he saw us now—"

"I have an agreement with him," Emily interrupted, her voice tinged with new excitement. "I can have any of my friends visit me, or I can visit them. Including you."

The boy's eyebrows shot up. "Really?"

"Not only that, but I'm waiting right now to talk to William about teaching you and Julie."

"Isn't that a great idea?" Julie said to Gideon.

"Sure is!" He beamed with anticipation, then quickly frowned. "But when will you know for sure?"

Emily said, "In a few minutes, I hope." She glanced over her shoulder at the big house. "William should be ready to see me about now. I'll let you know."

The girls waved good-bye and hurried away, but Gideon heard Julie whisper, "What if my brother says no?"

Gideon didn't hear the answer, but he abruptly had to face the possibility that it might not work out. This caused an instant ache in his heart unlike any he had ever known before.

For a moment longer, Gideon stood staring after the girls; then he started jogging toward his home, dreading having to tell his mother about the stolen mule.

★ ★ ★ ★ ★

Nat's clumsiness in breaking the cook's oil lamp had prompted her to have the mistress banish Nat to hoeing in her vegetable garden. Orpheus worked beside him.

In a few minutes, Nat's hands blistered from using the heavy slave hoe. In all his fourteen years, he had never had to work like a field-hand slave. Assigned to his first master when they were both about five years old, Nat had been trained as a house servant. Once a teen, he had become William Lodge's body servant. Now he was a fugitive working for another white planter while waiting for William to come and return him to Briarstone.

Leaning the hoe's handle against his shoulder, Nat glanced at his blistered and bleeding palms. "Orpheus, how can you stand this?"

"I shouldn't even speak to you," he grumbled. "You're to blame for me being out here instead of in the kitchen, where I could sneak a bite of food now and then."

Nat said, "You should not have let the cook see you grinning when she smacked me with that big ladle."

"Just keep hoeing," Orpheus replied gruffly.

Nat forced his fingers to again close around the hoe handle. It was made of hickory, the knots knocked off and scraped with glass to make them smooth. The blacksmith had hammered the blade from heavy pig iron. Broad as a shovel, the hoe was very heavy to lift.

Nat kept trying to win the other youth's confidence so he could learn what he needed to know about a coffle chain. "Orpheus," Nat said, "you told me that you had once worked in the fields. I'd still like to know how you stand doing such hard work."

"You really want to know?" the other youth asked, stopping to wipe perspiration from his brow.

"I sure do. If you don't tell me how you stand this, my hands are going to be so torn up I can't hold the handle. That doesn't count the ache in my shoulders. It would be terrible if you had to finish this alone."

Orpheus scowled at Nat. "I hate to admit that you may be right, so I'll tell you. But you must promise to never tell anybody else."

"I hurt so much I promise."

"Good." Orpheus glanced about, but there was no one else

★ ★

around. Still, he lowered his voice. "Mistress tells me we're all going to be free. That's why I can stand being a slave for now."

"How does she know that?"

"I don't know, but she does. She and her husband don't see eye to eye on this. Maybe that was from being born in the North and coming here after they were married. Maybe that's why she taught me and some of the others to read in spite of her husband's disapproval."

"Freedom?" Nat asked, deliberately sounding doubtful. He was suspicious of Orpheus, recalling that the old carriage driver at Briarstone had told him before Nat ran away, *"Don't trust anyone, not even another slave. Some will betray you to the master for a trinket."*

"Don't scoff!" Orpheus snapped. "Almost every single one of our people has nothing to look forward to except hard work from the day he's born until he dies. But I dream of being free, and that's how I live. In hope."

Nat certainly identified with that. In spite of his misgivings, he felt that the youth had spoken the truth. "I hope you do make it to freedom, Orpheus."

Both returned to their work. The broken blisters on Nat's hands and the deep ache in his shoulders grew more painful with each rise and fall of the great hoe.

Maybe, he told himself, *he's beginning to soften toward me. If I can just think how to phrase the words, he might tell me what I need to know to free Rufus before he gets so far away that neither of us can escape our bonds.*

★ ★ ★ ★ ★

Although it was not yet noon when Gideon told his mother about the mule, she sent Kate to ring the big yard bell that brought Fletcher running from the fields. He listened in silence while Gideon repeated his story.

Fletcher thoughtfully stroked his chin. "It was likely that same person who raided the smokehouse last night. I trailed him to the edge of the swamp where he had built a campfire and left part of a bacon rind. But I think he's a city man. Otherwise he wouldn't have camped where the swarms of mosquitoes would bite him so much."

"Come to think of it," Gideon mused, "the way that fellow rode Hercules showed he wasn't used to that. He was bouncing like a button on a barn door."

Fletcher said, "I don't think he's a regular thief, or he would have taken more than one slab of bacon."

"Well, he can certainly sell our mule for a goodly price, Mr. Fletcher!" Mrs. Tugwell exclaimed.

Gideon realized his mother was so upset that she had spoken sharply. He quickly said, "I'm the one to blame, not Mr. Fletcher."

Her tone softened. "I didn't mean to snap at you, Mr. Fletcher," she apologized. "Losing that mule . . ." She checked herself when her voice broke.

"It's all right, Mama," Gideon said, putting his arms around her shoulders as she turned her face away.

"We'll manage, Martha," Fletcher assured her in a quiet, confident tone.

Gideon raised an eyebrow at Fletcher's informal use of his mother's first name.

"Really, John?" she asked, turning toward him, her eyes misted.

Gideon cocked his head at this second unexpected use of a first name, but he said nothing.

"Really, Marth—uh . . . Mrs. Tugwell." Fletcher quickly lowered his eyes as if he was embarrassed. "I'll notify the patrollers. While they're looking for runaway slaves, they might come across Hercules or our thief."

Gideon noticed that his mother seemed relieved. He said, "So don't worry, Mama. As I told Emily, things will work out all right."

"Tonight," his mother said, "you'll have to tell me all about her. But right now I'm very concerned about the man who stole Hercules. Do you suppose he really was a Yankee deserter?"

Gideon shrugged and looked at Fletcher, who said, "Could be a deserter, but maybe he's just some Yankee from the city who got separated from his command. Or he might be wounded or hurt and is just trying to stay alive until he finds another regiment."

★ ★

"At least he's not a prisoner," Mrs. Tugwell said. "Like Isham was."

"But they *let* him escape," Gideon reminded her. "At least, Brice, that friend of Emily's, made it possible for him to slip away. Brice took a big risk doing that."

"Yes. I suppose his superiors would have considered it almost like treason," Mrs. Tugwell mused. "Anyway, I shall always be grateful that Isham got away."

Fletcher stood up. "Maybe I'd better let the work go for now and try to find some patrollers. It'll be slow going on foot."

"I'll go with you," Gideon said, standing.

"I'd like the company," the man replied with a grateful smile, "but I noticed that hog has been rooting around the bottom of his pen so much that he might possibly get out. I was going to fix it tonight, but if you don't mind, Gideon . . ."

"Oh!" his mother exclaimed, "by all means, fix it now, Gideon! Lilly was playing so close to him today that he ran against the fence, trying to get at her. I've warned her so many times."

"I'll do it right away, Mama," Gideon said.

Fletcher opened the back door and stepped out onto the porch as Gideon bent to give his mother a quick peck on the forehead.

"Well, now!" Fletcher cried. "Would you look at that?"

Gideon and his mother rushed out the door and stopped to stare.

Hercules, covered with foaming sweat but without a rider, trotted up the long path toward the barn.

★ ★

TWISTS AND TURNS IN FREEDOM'S ROAD

Emily and Julie stood at William's bedside. "A school?" he exclaimed. "The answer is no."

Emily was prepared for this reaction. "When I was in Richmond, I read that at the beginning of this war, three out of five Northern children aged eight to eighteen had to regularly attend school. But in the South, only one out of five free whites attended public school. Slaves can't even be taught—"

"I don't care!" William broke in. "No!"

Emily remained calm. "The plantation school closed when the teacher went off to the war. Your mother is not physically able to tutor Julie anymore, and nobody in this whole area is doing any teaching."

"I'll not have you teaching that poor white trash boy in this house!"

"His name is Gideon!" Emily interrupted sharply. "He's poor and white, but he's not 'trash.' Someday he's going to be somebody, and I want to help him!"

"You don't believe he can actually become an author!" William scoffed. "I've known him for years. Knew his father, too. He was a dirt farmer; that's all he knew how to do. His son is just like him. They lived hand to mouth while the old man was alive, and it's no better for them now. Gideon will never amount to anything! Besides, he's as mule-headed as his father was."

Emily wanted to shout her defense of Gideon, but she forced herself to speak quietly. "Is that your honest opinion, or is it just

★ ★

what you tell yourself because you couldn't get his father to sell their place to you, and now Gideon's mother won't sell, either?"

"You're out of line!" William yelled, suddenly shifting his position and instantly wincing in pain.

"I don't mean to be," Emily told him. "But as long as I do all the things you ask, then in my free time I would like to teach others what I've learned."

William gave her a cold, hard stare, but she met his eyes and held them without blinking. Slowly she noticed a change in them, as if he had just thought of something.

"Since you're only going to be here a short time," he said thoughtfully, "I suppose you could try it."

Julie let out a joyful little squeal and immediately clamped a hand over her mouth when her brother frowned.

"Thank you, William," Emily said. "I appreciate it. Now we'll let you rest."

"Hold on!" he said firmly. "What did Toombs say when you gave him my orders for today?"

"We had a little discussion, and everything's fine."

William half closed his eyes as though he doubted that. "Is it going to work out?"

"I feel sure it will."

He admitted, "I thought he would have you in tears."

Emily smiled with satisfaction. "Nothing like that."

"Don't be fooled, Emily," William warned. "It's not in his nature to be nice to field hands or females."

"Including Yankee girls," she replied, her smile widening. She turned to Julie. "Let's tell your mother and Mrs. Stonum, then see how quickly we can set up our little school."

She silently added, *And go tell Gideon.*

★ ★ ★ ★ ★

The Tugwells' two hounds flopped in the shade of the barn while Gideon finished walking the mule around the yard to cool him down. Gideon then led Hercules to the barn, fed him grain, and began to rub his sweaty hide with a tow sack. Mrs. Tugwell and Fletcher stood in the open doorway watching.

★ ★

Gideon told them, "I'd sure like to know how he got away from that thief."

His mother turned to the tall, slender man. "Mr. Fletcher has an idea about that."

"Well," Fletcher said, "it seems logical that whoever stole Hercules didn't know much about animals, so he rode him hard before he either fell off or got bucked off. Being a smart mule, Hercules came back to where he is well fed and treated kindly."

Mrs. Tugwell said, "I sure hope they catch that thief so we won't have our smokehouse raided again."

Fletcher commented, "Whoever he was is probably well out of this area by now. I'd be surprised if we had any more trouble from him."

"I hope you're right," Gideon replied.

"Well," his mother said, "when you're through there, I'd feel better if you and Mr. Fletcher reinforced that pigpen. I don't want that big hog to get loose."

"But, Mama," Gideon exclaimed, trying to put off any form of hated farm work, "I didn't finish telling you about seeing Emily at the fence line."

"I'd like to hear all about it," Mrs. Tugwell said, "but there's so much work to do around here and we've lost so much time already this morning. Why don't you save that until suppertime?"

"All right," he said reluctantly, dreading the thought of having to work in the sultry July weather.

"After that," his mother continued, "I'd like to have you two start building a shed near the house. Our little place is so crowded, I need that extra storage room without having to come way out here to the barn."

"I think we can get started on the shed in an hour or so," Fletcher volunteered.

"Good!" Mrs. Tugwell said. "I'll get the drawings my husband made last year." She started to turn around when both hounds suddenly leaped up, bayed in their deep voices, and ran across the yard toward the long lane.

"Now, who in the world. . . ?" Gideon began, hurrying to the door.

★ ★

His mother exclaimed, "Why, it's Emily and Julie! They're turning in here!"

Gideon reached the barn door and looked down the lane past the running dogs.

A horse and buggy with Emily driving had just turned off the public road. Julie sat beside her on the single seat. Gideon hurried to meet them, wondering why they had come.

★　★　★　★　★

By midmorning, Nat's shoulders and arms ached so much that he could barely lift the broad, pig-iron slave hoe. He had wrapped his blistered hands with a piece torn from his shirttail, but nothing eased the burning pain of his bleeding palms.

In spite of all his mother had taught him about winning being in the mind and not the muscles, doubts invaded his thoughts. He tried to focus on getting coffle information from Orpheus.

"You say you've seen these drovers pass by here before?" he asked.

"Sure have. One time the master talked to them when they stopped to rest by the roadside. The master told us because I think he wanted to scare us so we wouldn't even think of running away."

"Told you what?"

"The drovers are former patrollers who were so mean to the fugitives they caught that planters hired them to walk some of our people to the Deep South. The drover you saw the day you were captured, the one with both a whip and pistol, is called Duff. Hollis has only a whip but no gun."

Nat considered this further complication to his plans of rescuing Rufus. Even if Nat did learn the one time his brother might be freed from the coffle chain, a gun in the hands of a mounted drover was an awful danger.

If the brothers did manage to flee without getting shot, Rufus would still be wearing iron cuffs with a short chain linking his wrists together. How could they get them off? Common sense told Nat there was no way to rescue his brother, yet he kept thinking of how to do the impossible.

Nat couldn't really afford to wait any longer before trying to

★　★

escape from the Trumble place, but what good was there in that if he didn't have an idea of how to free him from the coffle chain?

Orpheus broke into Nat's thoughts. "If you're still thinking about your brother, forget him. By now, he's been walked a hundred miles or so. Even if you could escape from here, it'd take you several days to catch up to the coffle. That's assuming some patrollers didn't catch you and beat you half to death. You're better off waiting here for your master to come claim you."

"I'm not so sure about that," Nat said doubtfully, forcing his screaming muscles to keep raising and dropping the hoe into the soil. "He whipped me once, just before I ran away. This time he'll want to make an example of me to the others. If I live, he'll probably sell me down the river so far, I could never escape again."

"Do you know how very few of our people ever reach freedom, even if they escape for a while? Like you: You got away from your master for a while, and then my master caught you. The road to freedom isn't for us."

Nat admitted, "It's full of surprise twists and turns, but it's worth taking."

"No, it's not. There's no real escape until we die."

Nat replied emphatically, "I'm going to die free."

"You're going to die in chains!" Orpheus declared. "So's your brother, and me, too."

Nat didn't reply. He remembered Orpheus telling of living in hopes of being free. Now Nat suspected Orpheus had just been talking, that he was afraid to take the risks involved in running away.

Nat recalled when he had been captured by Trumble. Rufus had seen him and grinned in recognition just before Nat was struck by Trumble's cane. Nat's precious freedom was snatched away and he was again in slavery, but his mind was still free.

His tortured muscles and burning hands claimed his attention again, and the dreams of freedom faded. Still, for the first time, he had said aloud, "I'm going to die free." That hopeful call reached through his pain. *I am going to die free!* he silently vowed. *So is Rufus.*

Nat abruptly stopped hoeing and stared off into the distance,

★ ★

mentally resolving the idea. It touched his heart, urging him to act.

I don't dare wait any longer, he warned himself. *I didn't know how to save Rufus when I started following his coffle, so delaying isn't going to help.*

"What's the matter with you?" Orpheus repeated.

Slowly Nat turned to face him. "Nothing's the matter," he said calmly. "Nothing at all." But in his mind he and Rufus were already on the freedom road.

★ ★ ★ ★ ★

Emily and Julie sat grinning at Gideon in the shade of the Tugwells' front porch. Gideon's mother and Fletcher smiled at him, but his face was somber.

"It sounds too good to be true," he said in a doubtful tone. "I don't like to be suspicious, but I just can't see William letting me come to Briarstone." He turned to Emily. "What do you think his reason is?"

"I hope I'm not speaking out of turn," she said, "but I think he figures he can keep an eye on you while you're at our classes and then try to persuade you to convince your mother to sell this farm to him."

"I can't sell it," Mrs. Tugwell said. "Not that I would anyway. This land is all my family has to earn a living. Besides, my husband is buried here. Emily, you may not know this, but under Virginia law, women can use the family property to support themselves, but we can't own it in our own names. So my stepson, Isham, who's in the army, really owns this farm."

Emily exclaimed, "You can't own this land?"

"No," Mrs. Tugwell replied, "widows are only life tenants. My late husband owned this farm before we were married, but if it had been mine, by law, the moment I married, I would have surrendered everything to him."

Emily looked at Gideon. "Did you know this?"

"Yes, and so does William because we discussed this almost a year ago. But Mr. Fletcher can probably explain the law better than I can."

★ ★

When Emily's gaze turned to him, he nodded. "The husband has absolute custody and control of a couple's children. According to law, he can even beat her if the stick is no thicker than his thumb."

Emily admitted, "I don't know much about any state law, but this is really hard to believe."

"It's true," Gideon's mother said. "Because a woman can't own property, she can't make any transactions about property. She also can't make a will—or buy, sell, or free a slave, either. Not that I ever had a slave."

"So," Gideon explained, "William would be wasting his time trying to get me to tell Mama to sell this farm. He would have to convince Isham, and he's off fighting the war someplace. We don't even know where."

Emily lightly tossed her head so that the curls rippled down her back. "Then why did William agree to let you come to Briarstone so I can help with your writing?"

Gideon glanced at Fletcher before answering. "Julie, does Barley Cobb come to see your brother very often?"

"Yes, sometimes. William pays him to catch servants who have run away. Why do you ask?"

Gideon hesitated, suspecting that William had some plan in mind about getting Cobb to marry Gideon's mother, gain control of the farm, and then sell it to William. Gideon had no idea how that might be done, but he was sure that this goal was behind William's decision to let him come to Briarstone for tutoring.

Finally Gideon told Emily, "I can't say anything more."

"But there's no reason you shouldn't come to our little school, is there?"

"I guess not. In fact, I'd give anything to learn more about writing and spelling."

"Good!" Emily gave everyone a widening smile. "Then as soon as Julie and I can get things together, we'll let you know when it starts."

"It'll have to be in the evening," Gideon said hurriedly. "There's too much work to do around here in the daytime."

"Evenings are fine," Emily assured him. She stood and

★ ★

brushed off her skirt. "Someday when you're a famous writer, I want to know Julie and I had some small part in helping you reach your goal."

His blue eyes met her violet ones in silent gratitude. Whatever hidden reason William had for letting him come to Briarstone, Gideon had to risk it to get the help he needed to write better.

Even though he felt some concern, he smiled shyly at Emily. "I can hardly wait to get started," he told her.

★ ★

HEY, YANKEE GIRL!

The black hog's pen was reinforced with stout stakes driven deep into the ground below the last board rail.

Gideon straightened up and slid the heavy hammer into his belt. "There, now," he told Fletcher with satisfaction, "I don't think he'll be able to root those stakes out and crawl under the fence."

"I think you're right," Fletcher said. "The only way this boar can get out is if someone leaves the door open to his shed. The latch is too high for your sisters to reach, and Ben's old enough to know better. So your mother doesn't need to be concerned anymore."

Wiping sweat from his brow with the back of his tanned hand, Gideon glanced at the sun still high in a hot, sultry sky. He would have preferred being in the shade of the barn, writing on one of his stories, but there were higher priorities.

"I guess we'd better start building that shed for Mama," he said. "Papa laid some timbers aside for that last year. Should we hook up Hercules to the sled and haul them all at once or a few at a time as we need them?"

"First, I suggest we go over the plans and make sure your mother still wants the shed by the smokehouse."

Nodding, Gideon followed Fletcher to the back porch, where Mrs. Tugwell had left the plans on the top step. Gideon could hear his sisters playing in their room and his mother working in the kitchen.

★ ★

"Seems strange not to hear her singing," Gideon said softly while Fletcher studied the plans in the shade of the back porch. "Especially hymns. She knew them all, but since Papa died, she says she's been too sad to sing."

"Sadness takes a long time to pass, Gideon."

"How long does it take?"

"I don't know. I'm still finding out."

Gideon thought about Fletcher's wife, son, and brother dying before he joined the Confederate militia. Fletcher had been in the same regiment as Isham, Gideon's older half brother. He had been wounded at Manassas, and Fletcher had lost his left hand there.

"I miss Papa," Gideon confessed, "but not like Mama does, and not like you must miss your wife."

Fletcher didn't seem to hear. He folded the rough plans Gideon's father had hand drawn. "I think this will be a simple job. Would you mind stepping inside and asking your mother exactly where she wants this built?"

Gideon sighed, thinking how hard it was to get two lonely grown-ups to think the way he wanted. "Be right back," he said and turned toward the back door.

"Hmm? Who's that?" Fletcher asked quietly.

Gideon turned to follow the direction of Fletcher's extended right hand. "I don't see anything," Gideon said.

"Down there by the little hill where your father's buried. See? Someone's moving there, crouched down."

Gideon squinted until he could make out a man half hidden by brush. "That's Cobb!" Gideon exclaimed. "What's he doing on our place? Spying! Trying to get something on you or me so he can bring the rangers down on us!"

"You stay here," Fletcher said. "I'll go have a little talk with Mr. Cobb."

"I want to go with you."

"I think your mother would prefer you to stay here. I'll be back shortly," Fletcher said and strode off on long legs.

For a moment, Gideon watched in uncertainty; then he turned quickly and rushed into the kitchen. "Mama! Barley Cobb is

★ ★

sneaking around over by the graveyard, and Mr. Fletcher is heading straight for him!"

"Oh my stars!" Martha Tugwell exclaimed, whipping off her apron. "You stay here with your brother and sisters until I get back." She rushed out the door.

Gideon started to protest, but she called to Fletcher, who was already behind the barn and out of sight. Mrs. Tugwell lifted her long skirts just above her shoe tops and broke into an awkward jog after Fletcher. Gideon remembered the stories he had heard about how brutal and mean Cobb was when he caught runaway slaves. What would he do to a one-handed man he resented as much as he did Fletcher?

★　★　★　★　★

Emily and Julie approached Mrs. Stonum where she had sought to escape the sultry weather under the shade of a great spreading oak. She fanned herself, having earlier declined Anna Lodge's offer of a personal attendant to do that. Mrs. Stonum smiled in greeting as the girls stepped through the English box hedge and sat down on a stone bench across from her.

"Guess what Julie and I are going to do?" Emily began, returning the widow's smile.

"Mrs. Lodge told me you're going to start a school."

Emily was only a little disappointed that she hadn't been able to surprise Mrs. Stonum.

"When Julie told me the plantation school had been closed ever since the teacher went off to war," Emily said, "and Aunt Anna doesn't feel well enough to tutor anymore, I thought it would be fun to have a little school right here."

"My brother has approved it," Julie said hastily. "He's even going to let Gideon attend."

"I see." Mrs. Stonum stopped fanning herself. "I know you're a bright young woman, Emily, and I remember you telling me long ago that you taught your brothers back in Illinois."

"And Sunday school," Emily added quickly. "Of course, I taught younger ones there, but I found that I loved it. Our pastor said I was a natural-born teacher."

"I'm not surprised," the woman said. "I also understand that, generally, Northern education is ahead of our Southern ways. But where will you get books and supplies? The way the Yankee blockade has stopped us from getting so many items from outside—"

"The Bible and newspapers!" Julie broke in. "It's Emily's idea. Not only can we practice reading from them, but learn spelling, write reports, and do other things."

A faint smile tugged at the widow's lips. "It's nice to see someone get excited about learning. Maybe having the plantation school closed all this time will have some benefit after all. That will keep you occupied until we have to leave for Illinois in September."

"No, late August," Emily corrected. "I want to leave about ten days early so that if something unexpected happens, there'll still be time to get across the Potomac before our passes expire on September fifth. Is that all right with you?"

"Of course," the widow replied, fanning again. "But I've decided that I should return to Richmond until then. I can't nurse the wounded with a broken arm, but I can comfort or read to the wounded in the hospitals."

Mrs. Stonum glanced at Julie and added quickly, "Of course, in happier times, I would be glad to stay on and continue to enjoy the hospitality here. But all of you will be busy, and I am not used to sitting around."

"You could nurse my brother," Julie suggested.

"I am not trained in treating spinal problems," the widow replied. "Besides, it's my understanding that the doctor says only time will heal William's injuries."

Emily felt some anxiety that her traveling companion might not return in time. "I can understand how you feel, Mrs. Stonum, but making that trip to Richmond and then back here again, plus all the way to Illinois, not to mention your having to then go back to your own home, will be very hard on you. Are you sure?"

"Quite sure," she said. "I think it's best. . . ." She let her voice trail off as she looked behind the girls. "Someone's coming," she said.

Emily turned to see a rider wearing a wide planter's hat. "Oh,"

★ ★

she explained, "that's Mr. Toombs, the overseer. He's probably coming to report on the day's work so I can pass it on to William."

"He looks sort of angry," Julie observed.

"I don't think he likes dealing with me any more than he did you, but he has no reason to be angry," Emily told her. "Excuse me. I'll go meet him." She stood up and walked from the shade of the tree into the sunshine.

"Hey, Yankee girl!" he yelled, his face dark with anger. "I want to talk to you!"

Startled, Emily stopped dead still.

Behind her, she heard Julie say under her breath, "Oh no! Now what?"

★　★　★　★　★

Having made up his mind to escape from Trumble as soon as possible, Nat turned his thoughts to when and how that could best be done. He was certain he could flee this plantation, but logically, he knew he had no chance of saving his younger brother. Still, Nat's heart ached for Rufus, and emotion began to replace all sense and judgment.

I have to try, Nat kept reminding himself. *No matter how hard it seems, I can't just do nothing. So I've got to try.* He took a deep breath and silently added, *Even if we die, we'll die free.*

His concentration was so intense that he ignored the fierce pain in his blistered, bloody palms and the throbbing agony of his arms, shoulders, and back. The huge slave hoe had become a deadweight, but he managed to keep it rising and falling in the garden soil.

He was vaguely aware of hearing a bugle begin its plaintive call. The unique notes disrupted his intense concentration. He leaned the hickory handle against his shoulder and listened intently to the bugle.

He glanced at Orpheus, who was also listening.

Nat asked, "Isn't that the same melody we heard at night from the Yankee camps across the river?"

"Same one," Orpheus agreed.

Nat mused, "But I thought your master said that the Union

★　★

played that after 'Tattoo' and replaced 'Lights Out' with this music."

"He did, but this bugler is close by, at that Confederate camp this side of the river." Orpheus glanced at the sky, the sun still far from the horizon. "At church service the other night in the woods, one of the field hands told me he had seen some Confederates burying their dead out of their camp. Then their bugler played that same music at the end of the short service."

"You think that's what they're doing now?"

"Must be. Sure sounds sad and lonely, doesn't it?"

"Very," Nat agreed. "But it also feels sort of right for a soldier's funeral."

"Well, they won't play it over you and me," Orpheus mused, returning to his hoeing. "I guess it's only for white folks—no matter which color uniform they wear."

I'm half white, Nat thought, forcing his tender hands around the hoe handle, *but because my mother was black, the law says I'm black, too. A black slave.*

He shook his head to rid himself of the melancholy feeling the bugler had given and to stop the negative thoughts about being a slave.

I'm going to be free, he reminded himself. *No matter what color folks say I am, I'm going to be free.* With great effort, he lifted the hoe and let it fall. *Maybe tonight. And soon—somehow—Rufus will also be free.*

Nat ignored a second thought: *Or we'll both be dead.*

★　★　★　★　★

The overseer reined in his horse and glowered down at Emily, who stopped beside him. He growled, "I just found out that some of the blacks heard you being saucy with me this morning," he began, "and they laughed."

"I'm sorry, Mr. Toombs."

"Being sorry doesn't help!" he snapped. "Miss Emily, I don't care if you are young Master William's cousin, I will not be made a fool of in front of those people! So I whipped the boy who started it, and I'd like to do the same to you. But instead, I'm going to

★　★

warn you: Don't ever sass me again in front of those blacks! That clear?"

She involuntarily drew back. No one had ever spoken to her in such a rude way. But she quickly recovered her composure, knowing Julie and Mrs. Stonum had heard him.

"Sir," she replied coolly but firmly, trying to disregard the sharp increase in her heart rate, "I said I was sorry. I will not again offend you that way. I expect you to grant me the same courtesy!"

His face contorted with contempt. "And if I don't, what will you do? Run to William so I'll lose my job?"

"No, Mr. Toombs. This problem is between you and me. I won't bother William with it."

He seemed not to hear. "I can get a job anyplace. Because of the war, there's a shortage of good overseers at many plantations."

"You weren't listening!" she said resolutely. "You and I will have to work this out between us."

"There's nothing to work out," he replied harshly.

"Oh, but there is! You have a job to do, and so do I. Now, I intend to do mine, but it would be easier for both of us if we did it in a friendly way."

He raised an eyebrow. "Meaning what?"

"We should be cooperative and understanding."

He stared down at her with domineering eyes, but she met them and did not blink or look away. Finally he gave his head a quick little shake, and a smile touched his hard face. "Well, I suppose we could try again."

"Thank you, Mr. Toombs."

He bobbed his head and turned the horse around.

As he rode away, from behind her, Emily heard two loud, rushing sounds as if Mrs. Stonum and Julie had been holding their breaths and suddenly exhaled.

Emily quietly sighed. Her thoughts leaped ahead. *I don't want him to get upset with me again.* She returned to the shade of the tree, thinking, *I've got to do something that will make him easier to get along with. But what?*

★ ★ ★ ★ ★

★ ★

Gideon's siblings had been banished from the kitchen, where he watched his mother gingerly washing a small cut on Fletcher's face. He had vainly protested when she insisted he sit on the bench while she treated him.

"I think it will heal without a scar," she said.

Gideon tried again to get an answer to the question he had posed when they returned from the encounter with Cobb. "What happened out there?"

Fletcher shrugged. "When I told Cobb that he was trespassing on private property, he didn't say anything but just swung at me. I didn't duck fast enough."

Mrs. Tugwell scolded, "You should have waited for me to get there, Mr. Fletcher. He wouldn't have struck me."

"He won't strike me again, either," Fletcher replied grimly.

Gideon wanted to ask why, but his mother anticipated his question and gave him a warning look, saying, "I don't imagine he'll be back."

"At least not alone," Fletcher guessed. "Next time, he'll bring the rangers with him."

"He'll have no reason to do that," Mrs. Tugwell said angrily, lowering the wet cloth and stepping back.

"He'll find one," Fletcher answered, rising from the bench. "Thank you, Martha. You've got a gentle touch."

"Don't mention it," she said, suddenly fluttering her hands in a way Gideon had never seen before.

"Anyway, I'm obliged," Fletcher assured her. "Come on, Gideon. Let's get back to work."

As the door closed behind them, Gideon was surprised to hear his mother start softly humming.

★ ★

UNCERTAIN WELCOME AT BRIARSTONE

After carefully considering the safest time to escape from Trumble, Nat chose a Sunday. Many plantations made that a day of rest for the slaves, but church was often mandatory. In the morning, the master and mistress rode their carriage to the village house of worship.

Nat and Orpheus walked the four miles there with the other barefoot field hands and household staff members. All carried their shoes. Nat's blistered hands hurt from the weight of the shoes, but he ignored the pain. Leather footwear would be useful in woods, brush, and briars.

Orpheus asked, "Why're you looking around all the time?"

Nat had studied the surrounding countryside, noting stands of trees and creeks where he hoped to hide from both patrollers and slave catchers with tracking bloodhounds.

"I'm just enjoying looking at something besides the plantation," Nat said innocently.

"Looking is all you're going to be able to do," Orpheus declared in a low tone. "You won't get more than a few miles before they catch you."

Nat dropped his voice so the others walking and talking nearby could not hear. "You don't know what I'm thinking, Orpheus. But if you did, and you were right, the master probably might suspect you were involved. That could get you whipped." He paused before adding, "So you don't really have any idea of what I'm thinking, do you?"

★ ★

Orpheus's eyes widened in understanding of what Nat meant. "No, you're right. I hadn't thought of that."

"Now you can."

Orpheus silently walked on for a moment before sidling closer to Nat. "Don't look now, but when you can, look toward the creek. In that clearing among the trees there's a barn. The man who owns it helps runaways get on the Underground Railroad. But if you ever tell anyone I said that, I'll call you a liar and get you whipped."

Nat wasn't sure whether Orpheus spoke the truth or if he was baiting a trap. Nat decided to at least fix the barn's location in his memory just in case.

At the church door, Nat joined the other slaves in putting on their shoes. They climbed up to the balcony to sit on backless, rough wooden benches. The July heat, trapped below the low ceiling, soon had each worshiper sweating freely. Nat was aware that each also warily watched wasps buzzing by on their endless trips to and from their nests about a foot or two overhead.

Nat ignored the stinging insects to concentrate on making final plans for his escape. That would have to be tonight, under cover of darkness. He would need grease and black pepper from the kitchen to smear on his shoes and legs. He had done that when he and the slave girl named Sarah had escaped from Briarstone. He would also need food, but taking that from under the sharp eyes of the fat black cook might arouse suspicion.

While he mentally worked out the final details of escape, he was careful to keep up a proper outward appearance. He joined in singing hymns with the white congregation seated in cushioned pews below. He seemed to earnestly gaze at the white preacher when he rose to deliver his expected sermon. As usual, it included a warning to the balcony worshipers to work hard and obey their masters. But Nat didn't really listen.

When the service was over and he was again walking barefoot back toward the Trumble plantation, Nat could hardly wait for nightfall to start looking for Rufus.

★ ★ ★ ★ ★

★ ★

After changing out of his Sunday clothes and into his work ones, Gideon returned to the barn for a private talk with Fletcher. He had finished removing bales of hay from the wagon. Covered with an old horse blanket, the bales had served as seats for Gideon's mother, brother, and sisters on the ride to and from church.

"How's your face?" Gideon asked, taking one end of the horse blanket to help fold it.

"Healing fine, thanks to your mother's care."

It was an opening that Gideon had not expected so easily, but he pounced on it. "When we were coming back from Richmond after selling our summer wheat, you said something that I still remember."

Fletcher took the folded blanket and placed it on a shelf near the mule's stall. "Oh? What was that?"

"Well, I was saying that I was glad Mama wouldn't have to marry Cobb because we'd sold the wheat for enough that we could all live through the winter. Remember?"

When Fletcher nodded, Gideon continued. "Then you said, 'Your mother is a very fine woman.' Remember that?"

Fletcher half closed his eyes, looking suspiciously at the boy. "Yes, because she is."

Gideon hesitated, unsure of how to pursue his goal but determined to push ahead. "She used to sing all the time. Mostly hymns, but she hadn't even hummed since Papa died. After she washed your face from where Cobb hit you, I heard her humming. She was doing it again this morning when we were getting ready for church."

"I'm glad, Gideon." Fletcher sat down on the edge of a manger. "She deserves another chance at being happy."

Words leaped to Gideon's lips, but he held them back, uncertain if he should say them aloud. He perched beside Fletcher and decided to speak. "If you go away, I'm afraid she'll stop humming and maybe never sing again."

A faint hint of a smile tugged at the man's lips. "You think I don't know what you're driving at, Gideon?"

Dropping his eyes, Gideon confessed, "Maybe."

★ ★

He looked up when the strong right hand closed firmly but gently on his shoulder. "Then you won't go?"

For several seconds, there was no answer. Fletcher's face was somber when he finally spoke. "I hate to leave you with all the responsibility of this farm, but if we don't stop the Yankees before they get here, they'll take your crops, the animals, the chickens—everything. I've got to go help stop those invaders."

Gideon's eyes dropped to Fletcher's left wrist stub.

He said, "I know, Gideon. But even with one hand, I can do something. As long as that Yankee General Pope is doing such terrible things to my former friends and neighbors in the valley, I've got to go help them."

Gideon's personal objective was too strong to accept any reason that Fletcher could offer. "When you're gone," he cried in fading hope, "Barley Cobb will be back! He'll pester Mama something fierce!"

Fletcher closed his eyes and winced as though in pain, replying, "Before I go, I'll have another little talk with Cobb so he won't bother your mother."

"But you don't know him the way I do! He'll probably say anything to you, but if you're not around, mark my words, he'll be back. He told me flat-out that he's going to marry Mama, and I couldn't stand that."

Fletcher's eyes opened, but pain showed in them. "I wish I could say something that will ease your mind, but I can't. After harvest this fall, I've got to go back."

Gideon was too disappointed and heartsick to answer. Without a word, he hurried out of the barn. He quickly passed the hogpen, ignoring the boar as it threw itself against the fence. Gideon strode across the fields toward the swamp. He stopped at the edge, overcome by his emotional pain. Then he shook his head.

I can't quit, he rebuked himself. *Mama's happiness depends on it.*

★　★　★　★　★

That afternoon, while Orpheus was again occupied in talking with the fifteen-year-old house maid, Nat slipped into the kitchen

★　★

when the fat cook was at the smokehouse. Nat gathered the pepper and grease in two separate containers. He wrapped them and his shoes in a tow sack, made sure nobody was watching, then eased into the woods.

Near the slave's secret hush-arbor, he hid his supplies under a downed log, then returned to the plantation.

★　★　★　★　★

When dusk spread soft shadows over the plantation, Nat was delighted that Orpheus was so enthralled with the girl. Nat trailed them and arrived after dark at the slaves' secret place of worship in the woods. One woman was already shouting with her head in the kettle while others waited to take their turn.

Nat sat in the back row, ignored by Orpheus and the girl. That suited Nat fine. He waited until the singing and handclapping started and many eyes were closed.

Nat quietly slipped away without anyone noticing. With his heart beating faster in excitement, Nat put on his shoes, carried the sack with the two containers, and disappeared into the night.

★　★　★　★　★

By Tuesday of Emily's second week at Briarstone, she and Julie had gathered all the newspapers that Uncle George had brought from the village, including ones published in Richmond plus one rare copy of a Union daily. Headlines on every front page screamed the latest news about the war's progress.

Emily tapped the two papers she had spread out on the lawn under the great oak. "Both the North and the South tell the same story, but each one says the other army was defeated and their own troops won. Which one can we believe?"

"Mother told me what her father said about war when she last visited him. It was something like, 'In war, the first casualty is always Truth.' "

Emily thought about that while absently gazing around the endless green lawn. Several small black children were laughingly chasing white ones in a game of tag. It was a pleasant childhood scene, but something about it also troubled her.

★　★

"Speaking of truth," Emily said over her shoulder, "how is it that black and white children can play together, but when they get older, the whites often become the master or mistress and the black children are slaves without any rights?"

"That's just the way it is," Julie explained matter-of-factly. "Pickaninnies grow up to take their rightful place as servants to their superiors."

Emily whirled to face her cousin. "Pickaninnies? I thought that was considered an offensive word."

"When they get older, many people in the South call them worse names than that, like—"

"Don't say it!" Emily interrupted. "It's hard enough for me to hear them referred to as 'servants' when they really are slaves."

"Servant is a good word," Julie protested.

Emily could sense the conversation was getting into a sensitive area where neither girl would change her mind, but she couldn't help saying one more thing. "Why do you say that one race is superior to another?"

"Because everyone says so, that's why!" Julie's voice had taken on an annoyed edge. "I've even heard preachers say so from the pulpit."

Emily replied, "You sound just like Uncle Silas!"

"I learned it from him," Julie replied a bit defensively. "It's always been that way and always will be. Don't be so shocked."

Emily didn't want to quarrel, so she choked back the rebuttal that sprang to mind. Instead, she said, "I just can't believe that. President Lincoln seems determined to change that, too."

"He can talk all he wants, but he can't make the South do it just because he says so. Anyway, not all white children grow up to be masters. Many are like our overseer, Toombs—a poor white. His children and many others will grow up to be just like him: uneducated, lazy, undependable, and not much better than a slave."

"I've heard your father and brother both call Gideon 'poor white trash,'" Emily said. She wished that she could stop the conversation's awkward direction, but she strongly felt the need to

★ ★

stand her ground and defend Gideon, even with Julie, whom she loved dearly.

"Gideon's different," Julie admitted.

"In what way?"

Julie heaved an exasperated sigh. "Because he has ambition! Because he wants to be somebody—a writer. Because he's anxious to be educated, that's why."

Emily forced herself to take a deep breath and watch her words before answering. "Do you think education is the difference between being like Mr. Toombs' children and those black ones?"

Julie also took a deep breath before replying. "I don't know," she admitted, her tone level again. "Look at his six children. All they do all day long is play or go running around like wild deer. They went to school now and then before it closed. Toombs has been very upset since that happened."

Emily fell silent, thoughtfully watching the children. "Julie," she said, "I'm getting an idea."

"I'm afraid to ask what it is."

"You don't need to. Come on. I'll tell you about it while we look for Uncle George. I want him to carry a message to Gideon saying we'll hold our first class on Friday. Then I'll tell you what else I plan to do."

★　★　★　★　★

The following Friday at dusk, Gideon had never felt so out of place as he dismounted from Hercules. Wearing his Sunday clothes, with his hair combed and slicked down, he slowly passed between the white columns where a Confederate flag floated from its staff. At the massive front door, he rang the bell, having grave doubts about why William had given permission for him to be tutored at Briarstone. Gideon was suspicious, but at the same time, he was eager to see Emily and learn what she could teach him about becoming a writer.

He gave a final polish to the tops of his Sunday shoes by alternately running them against the back of his pant legs. He stopped in embarrassment when the ornate door opened and a slender, light-skinned man in a black suit haughtily looked down at him. He had the impression that the slave considered himself a superior.

"Use the back door," the man said coldly.

Gideon nodded and started to turn away.

"Jason," a girl's voice called from inside the house, "who is it?"

"A poor white laborer, I believe, Miss Julie."

The boy stopped and raised his voice. "It's Gideon."

"Gideon!" Julie rushed to the door. "You're a bit earlier than I expected. But come in! Come in! I'm sorry that I forgot to tell Jason you were expected."

Gideon stepped inside, now humiliated and even more unsure of himself. His eyes swept the room with its grand staircase, the Chippendale sofa with its gilding and fretwork, and a Louis XI armchair with its claw-and-ball feet. A tall case clock ticked against a wall near a large gilt-framed oil portrait of Julie's father. He seemed to scowl disapprovingly at Gideon.

He would have liked to leave at once, but Emily glided down the carpeted stairs, golden hair framing her flawless face, which was lit with a warm smile.

"Gideon!" she exclaimed. "I'm glad you came."

He nodded but couldn't think what to say.

Julie said, "My brother wants to talk to you."

Alarmed, Gideon blurted, "What about?"

"He didn't say. This way, please." She turned toward the stairs.

Gideon looked at Emily, who shrugged, indicating that she didn't know, either. Then she followed Julie.

Gulping anxiously, Gideon reluctantly trailed them.

THREATS BY A
YANKEE GENERAL

William did not smile when Gideon and the girls entered his bedchamber. He lay stretched out flat on the high bed while his young new body slave stood silent as a post against the back wall. William turned his head toward the visitors but kept his injured back still. His face was pale and drawn, yet his voice was strong.

"Sit down, everyone," he said.

Julie sank into the Boston rocker by the fireplace. Emily sat on the edge of the small settee in front of an open window. Gideon chose to stand, wary of why his longtime adversary wanted to see him.

It was the closest Gideon had ever been to him without getting pummelled. Gideon realized that he had grown taller and heavier since their last encounter. He sensed that even when William recovered, he would think twice before attacking again.

William gingerly moved his legs and winced with pain before focusing his hard eyes on Gideon. "I hope you know it's a privilege for you to be invited into this house."

Gideon heard Emily's sharp intake of breath, and a hot surge of resentment swept over him that he had been summoned here to be belittled in front of the girls. But Gideon forced himself to answer quietly. "I do, and I want to thank you for allowing me to come here to study."

William added, "I'm in a position to do a lot of things for you and your family. Keep that in mind."

He waved his hand in a casual gesture of dismissal, then

★ ★

turned toward his body servant. "Levi, you didn't get that lump out of the bedding under my right foot. Can't you do anything right?"

Gideon turned to go, his cheeks burning, but he needed to learn from Emily, so he walked out with his head held high. Behind him, he heard Emily say sharply under her breath, "Really, William! That was—" She broke off her words, loudly sighed, and rushed out of the room.

Gideon hurried down the stairs with both girls trailing him. Anger and humiliation caused the blood to pound in his ears, drowning out all other sounds. *I've got to have help with my writing!* he fiercely reminded himself. *So I'm not going to let him get the best of me!*

★　★　★　★　★

It was early evening of the sixth night since Nat escaped from the Trumble plantation, and he was so weary that he wanted to find a hiding place to sleep. But he could not do that. His stomach constantly reminded him that it had been two days since he last ate.

That had been only some cold cornbread and a pitcher of buttermilk. An old slave woman smoking a pipe had slipped that to him when he risked entering the quiet quarters of a small plantation while all the hands were in the fields. She had also given Nat hope. Through a mouth of missing teeth, she said a coffle with two white drovers had passed this way some days ago.

Nighttime was also the safest time to travel even though Nat had seen and heard white patrollers on horses moving through the darkness. Their lanterns, periodically held high in efforts to locate black runaways, had warned Nat to drop down and not move. He was grateful that none of the searchers had hounds that would follow his scent.

Continuing his quest and ignoring his empty belly, by moonrise he had entered the roadway he believed was the one his brother had been forced to take. By now Rufus was at least a hundred miles away, but he was in chains, and Nat had no encumbrances. He had thrown away the lard and black pepper because

★　★

even their relatively light weight hurt his blistered hands.

Rounding a curve, he caught the savory fragrance of meat cooking over an open fire. His stomach knotted at the delicious scent, but he ignored that to locate the source. He heard faint laughter from men in a stand of dark trees. Darting off the road, Nat dropped to the ground, alert to danger. Raising his head and crawling slowly forward, he spotted a campfire and four men about thirty yards away.

They're not soldiers, he decided after seeing two men walk in front of the flames. *They're white, but overweight and slow—too old to be drafted into the army. They must be patrollers, but they don't have any dogs with them.*

The sight of a rabbit roasting on a stick made his mouth water and his empty stomach lurch, but Nat quietly returned to the edge of the roadway. He didn't want to leave any more tracks that might be seen by a roving lantern light, so he stayed on the green grass. He took off and carried his heavy shoes so his bare feet would be noiseless while he tried to creep past the danger.

He froze when one of the men suddenly stood up and spoke loudly enough that Nat could hear. "What's taking Jed so long to get that water?"

Until then, Nat had not been aware of the barely audible sound of shallow water running over stones just ahead in the darkness. A small creek obviously flowed there, which meant the man who had gone for water might be anywhere near.

Where's his lantern? Nat wondered, peering anxiously toward the sound of the small stream. *Or could he have gone without a light?*

A slight rustling sound made Nat whirl around. By the thin light of the moon, he glimpsed a man rushing toward him.

"Bring a light!" the patroller shouted to his friends. "I got me a runaway black boy!"

"Naw, suh, you ain't!" Nat cried in dialect as he ducked under the man's arms, then darted into the night.

★　★　★　★　★

Emily and Julie had both apologized for William's rudeness

★ ★

when they first sat down in three upholstered chairs in Silas Lodge's dark-walled library. Gideon quickly brushed the incident aside to look at newspapers George had brought home from the village of Church Creek.

Emily turned to the teaching session. "I thought we could start by each of us reading aloud from one of these papers. Here are two Confederates: The *Richmond Examiner*, which I learned while living there is critical of both President Jeff Davis and Congress. The *Enquirer* here"—she pointed to the second paper—"usually defends the President. It's harder to get a Union paper, of course, but George found this copy of the *Baltimore American*. Do either of you have a preference?"

Julie said, "One of Father's letters said that this Yankee newspaper prints lies. I don't want to read it. And why couldn't George get a copy of the *Whig* or the *Dispatch*? Father says it's especially loyal to our boys."

"I'm grateful for what papers we have," Emily replied. "Gideon, which do you want?"

"Makes no difference to me."

"Then you take this one and I'll take the other." Emily said, handing over a paper. "Now, let's all pick a story, then take turns reading aloud. Is that all right?"

"Fine with me," Julie replied.

"Sure," Gideon said.

"After that," Emily continued, "we'll do the same with the Bible."

That held promise to Gideon because his mother had read it to him regularly since he was very young. The majority of his own reading had been done from the Bible, so he felt reasonably sure that he would do better reading that aloud to the girls.

Emily suggested, "Let's silently read straight through to each get our story in mind. Then, if there's a word that's hard to pronounce, or one we don't know, we can come back and study it. Is that all right?"

That being agreeable, each held the paper to the closest light and read in silence for five minutes.

★ ★

"Time's up," Emily announced with a smile. "Who wants to read first?"

Nobody did, so she began. "This issue is dated July eighteenth, a week ago today. 'Major General John Pope has announced that his Army of Virginia will subsist upon the country in which their operations are carried out.'"

Startled, Gideon blurted, "What?"

Emily lowered the paper to look across at him. "That's what it says. It goes on to say that citizens will be responsible for damage done by guerrillas to telegraph wires, railroads, and bridges. They will be compelled to repair any damage, plus—"

She stopped, glancing again at Gideon. "What's the matter?"

"Mr. Fletcher, the man who helps at our farm, will be very upset about that!"

Emily said, "Then he won't like this other story, either. Dated Monday of this week, the twenty-first, it says Union troops occupied Luray in the Shenandoah."

Gideon briefly closed his eyes, knowing that both stories might make Fletcher change his mind about waiting until autumn to leave. Then Mama would stop humming and maybe never sing again.

"I'm sorry, Gideon," Emily said. "If this upsets you, we'll read another story."

"No, it's all right," he said without conviction. "I just was surprised, that's all."

"Speaking of surprises," Julie said, rattling her paper as she placed it in her lap. "Here's one on the same subject. Just the day before yesterday, Wednesday, July twenty-third. 'Pope ordered that any man who refuses to take an oath to support the Union will be sent south. If he returns, he'll be treated as a spy.'"

"You're not serious?" Gideon exclaimed.

"See for yourself." Julie held out the paper to him.

As he reached for it, Emily suggested, "Why don't we all sit together on the sofa so we can see the story at the same time?"

Julie protested, "That's father's Louis XV winged sofa. It's very old."

"We'll be careful," Emily assured her. She gingerly sat down

★ ★

on the right, leaving room for Julie and Gideon.

He was reluctant, so rose slowly, which was a mistake. Julie promptly plopped down at the opposite end. That left only the middle between the girls for Gideon.

Squirming, he gingerly eased into that spot. It wasn't just that he had never been so close to young women before, but he was a slow, uncertain reader. Only his love of words and strong drive to be a writer kept him from making an excuse to leave. He didn't want to read aloud even though that's part of the reason he had agreed to attend the tutoring sessions. He thought of an excuse: He had to tell Fletcher about Pope's latest outrage.

Before he could bring himself to speak, Julie read aloud the next paragraph in her paper. " 'Any person who violates the oath will be shot and his property confiscated!' "

She threw the paper to the floor and leaped up, her eyes bright with anger. "Shot! Can you image what a beast that Pope is!" Without waiting for a reply, she turned to her cousin. "Emily, I love you with all my heart, but you're the only Yankee I would even speak to! If they're all like this General Pope—"

"They're not!" Emily broke in, her voice rising. "There are very fine, gentlemanly officers in the Union army! You can't judge them all by . . ." She let her voice trail off. In a quiet tone, she added, "Look what's happening to us! We're letting our emotions take over instead of studying! Let's start over, shall we?"

Gideon dropped his eyes, his mind racing with the news about Pope. Sooner or later, Fletcher would learn of the general's orders. Fletcher might change his mind about waiting until fall before leaving to help his former friends and neighbors in the Shenandoah Valley.

Gideon's eyes focused on another headline now facing up on the floor. He snatched the paper and skimmed the words. "Listen to this!"

He held it up so both girls could see. "It's dated Tuesday, July twenty-second, and says that President Abraham Lincoln has just issued a prelim . . ." he stumbled over the word, then thrust the paper into Emily's hands. "Here, you read it."

She glanced to where he pointed and continued. " 'He has just

★ ★

issued a preliminary edition of an emancipation proclamation that will free all slaves held in states now considered to be in Rebellion against the Union!' "

Julie cried, "He can't do that!"

Emily didn't answer but continued to scan the rest of the story. She said, "Apparently he's not going to make it official until sometime later, but it seems that he is really going to order that all slaves are to become free if they're in any of the Confederate states."

That was the end of the first lesson because the three readers again became involved in an emotional discussion about what they read and thought.

When Gideon mounted Hercules for the ride home, he hadn't learned much about how to write. However, he had bad news that would not be well received at home. Gideon leaned over the mule's withers and spoke aloud. "If Mr. Fletcher leaves, what will that do to Mama?"

★ ★ ★ ★ ★

The coal-oil lamps in the Tugwell kitchen burned late that night after everyone except Gideon and his mother had retired. Her old rocker squeaked steadily, indicating the depth of her distress. Gideon alternately moved from the homemade bench at the table to the chair that had been his father's favorite.

They somberly discussed the news Gideon had brought from Briarstone. When the lamp flame began to flicker as the fuel dropped below the length of the wick, his mother took a deep, shuddering sigh.

"We have no claim on Mr. Fletcher. He's a man of honor, so he will keep his word and not leave until the harvest this fall. But that would not be right. We must release him to do what he feels he must."

"But, Mama! He could get killed! You know he won't take that oath to the Union! Didn't you hear what I said about that Yankee general shooting—"

"I heard," she interrupted. "I . . . we . . . will miss him terribly. That'll throw all the hard farm work back on you and Ben. You may even be too tired to attend your school, but—"

"No!" Gideon jumped up from his father's chair. "I can't do that! I've got to learn, and there's nobody else in this whole area who can teach me except Emily!"

The lamplight reflected a sudden mist in his mother's eyes before she spoke again. "I know your heart wants to do that. But you already get up long before the rooster crows, and when Mr. Fletcher is gone, you'll be doing chores long after dark. You'll be so tired . . ."

"I've got to do it, Mama! I've just got to! Emily's only going to be here until the end of August!"

He knew his mother was fighting back tears, and that tore him up inside. He reached down and put both arms around her neck.

They stayed that way without speaking until the light flickered and started to go out.

"Tomorrow," she said softly, "we must give Mr. Fletcher our blessing to do what he feels he must."

She rose quickly, her eyes bright but her chin up. She kissed Gideon on the cheek. "Good night. Mama loves her big old boy."

Poor Mama! he thought as he blew out the final bit of flame and headed toward the bedroom he shared with Ben. *I wonder if she'll ever be happy again?*

★ ★

THE FUGITIVE

Nat rushed blindly through the night, hearing the shouts of the four white patrollers chasing him on foot. Even if they had horses picketed near their campfire, the brush and trees were too thick for horseback pursuit. This gave Nat hope for escape as he dodged among the trees, going away from the creek. Low-hanging branches whipped his face. His bare feet were cut by fallen limbs and twigs, but he kept running until his lungs seemed on fire and a stitch in his side forced him to stop.

Catching his ragged breath as quietly as possible, he located his pursuers by their bobbing lanterns and splashing of water. Nat realized with satisfaction that the men were following the creek, going away from him.

He glanced through an opening in the trees' canopy at the North Star. He was heading away from it, which meant he was still going south, the way his brother had traveled. Dropping his eyes, Nat was pleased to see the lanterns falling farther and farther behind.

When his breathing was controlled, he turned to walk on, not running for fear he would be heard. A vagrant breeze brought him another whiff of the roasting meat. His empty stomach constricted so hard that he flinched in pain. He stopped, sniffing, licking his lips.

With another glance at the lanterns, he turned toward the pale glow of the firelight. Easing through trees and brush, he vainly tried avoiding ground debris that painfully pierced his bare feet.

But the agony of his empty stomach and the fragrant lure of the abandoned meat drove him forward.

At the clearing, he paused, faintly hearing his pursuers in the distance and scanning the campfire. Not seeing anyone, he ran forward, frantic with hunger. He snatched the slanted stick that held a rabbit over the fire. He started to turn to run again, but something struck him hard on the back of the head. He felt his legs buckle. The last thing he remembered was falling down.

★ ★ ★ ★ ★

Gideon carried the lantern and milk pail to the barn before dawn and found Fletcher already feeding the stock.

"Morning, Gideon. How did the lesson go?"

"Fine." He avoided meeting the man's eyes, having made up his mind to say nothing about General Pope's harsh rules until breakfast. If his mother was present, it might influence Fletcher to stay on.

"Did you go straight to Briarstone last night?"

"Yes. Why?"

Fletcher stuck the pitchfork into the haymow before answering. "Because I heard a mule bray after you'd been gone awhile, so I got up and looked outside the barn. By what little moon there was, I saw a mule down by the fence. I didn't see a rider."

Gideon picked up the milking stool. "You think Cobb was sneaking around again?"

"Either that or another thief. But I've already checked the smokehouse and that new shed where your mother stores supplies. Nothing was taken."

Gideon sat down at the cow's right side and adjusted the bucket between his knees. "Didn't the dogs bark?"

"Your little brother took them hunting."

"Ben's not supposed to do that alone! He's too young! So it must have been Cobb who was sneaking around, in spite of the warning you gave him."

"Well, he's wasting his time." Fletcher picked up the shovel and started working on the floor. "He's not going to get anything on me, or you, either."

No, Gideon thought, *but he'll sure make it hard for both Mama and me if you leave.* Aloud, he said, "Mama was starting breakfast when I came out. She said for us not to be late because slapjacks have to be eaten hot."

Fletcher stopped shoveling and grinned. "We sure don't want to disappoint her, do we?"

I hope you don't, Gideon thought as he began milking. *But I'm sure you will when we tell you what that Yankee general is doing in the valley.*

★ ★ ★ ★ ★

Emily had trained herself to hear the sounding of the cow horn that roused field hands from their quarters. She dressed and hurried to where her cousin William was waiting to give her his daily orders to be relayed to Toombs, the white overseer.

"How did your class go last night?" he asked.

The question surprised her. "Well enough, I think." She had thought seriously about telling him of her strong objections to his rude remarks to Gideon. But in the interest of peace, she had decided to say nothing. She didn't want to discuss the tutoring session, either. So she promptly asked her daily question.

"What do you want me to tell Mr. Toombs to do today?"

"You ride sidesaddle, don't you?"

That was another question she hadn't expected. "Yes, some."

"Then today I want you to ride with Toombs into the fields and report to me what you see."

"But why? Every night I bring you his report—"

"I don't trust him or any overseer," William broke in. "Now, he won't like it, but he works for me. That's what I want done. You tell him. Then you ride with him and report to me tonight and every night. Is that clear?"

Emily swallowed hard and slowly nodded. She knew it was going to be a very bad day, with many more to follow.

★ ★ ★ ★ ★

Gideon and Fletcher sat down at the Tugwells' kitchen table as dawn began to break. Ben, Kate, and Lilly were still asleep.

★ ★

Gideon postponed the bad news about General Pope by suggesting that Fletcher tell about the mule down by the fence.

He nodded but waited until Mrs. Tugwell had served her generous-sized slapjacks and said the blessing before he repeated what he had earlier told Gideon.

His mother listened without comment until Fletcher had finished. Then she said, "I had hoped Mr. Cobb would stop trying to find something that he could use as an excuse to have the partisans come poking around. But, as the Good Book asks, 'Can the leopard change his spots?' Mr. Cobb will continue to be a thorn in our sides."

Gideon peered carefully at his mother, wondering if she was subtly trying to influence Fletcher before he learned about Pope's threat. But Gideon couldn't be sure, so he waited for her to take the lead.

"Did Gideon tell you about reading the newspapers last night at Briarstone?" she asked Fletcher.

"No, we talked of other things. Why?"

Gideon again made an effort to delay the inevitable. "Lincoln made a kind of preliminary announcement of plans to free all the slaves in the Confederacy."

"I'm not surprised." Fletcher glanced at his empty plate, then longingly at the stack of hot cakes from which faint wisps of steam still rose. "Martha, you are a real master at making great food."

"Have some more," she urged, reaching over to move the platter closer to him. "You and Gideon work so hard that you need lots of solid food to keep you going."

"Thanks. I believe I will." Fletcher lifted three more large cakes by the serving fork and settled them on his plate. He started to return the serving fork but seemed to sense something. Looking quickly from mother to son, he asked, "What's the matter? Did I take too many?"

"Oh no, of course not!" Mrs. Tugwell exclaimed. "There's plenty for everyone."

Fletcher's eyes narrowed slightly. "Then what am I missing?"

Mother and son exchanged glances before she nodded. "Tell him, Gideon."

★ ★

He didn't want to do it, but he took a deep breath and repeated the gist of the stories about General Pope's harsh orders and consequences for disobedience.

Fletcher didn't say a word or touch his food until Gideon had finished.

"I see," Fletcher said very quietly. "I see."

"Finish your breakfast, John," Mrs. Tugwell urged.

Fletcher looked at the fresh stack of cakes but did not pick up his fork. "I also see how this news affects you two, so let me put your minds to rest."

He looked first at Mrs. Tugwell, then at Gideon, before continuing. "It grieves me more than I can say to know these terrible threats have been made against my friends and neighbors."

Gideon's heart seemed to sink as he sensed what Fletcher was going to say next. Gideon saw that his mother's face was calm and composed. She obviously had prepared herself for Fletcher's leaving.

"But," he said, turning to look into Mrs. Tugwell's eyes, "I have given my word. I will stay here and help as best I can until after the harvest this fall."

"As a gentleman, I expected you would say that," she replied, her eyes steadily meeting his. "But Gideon and I talked last night, and we're agreed that you should do what you want. You have been honorable, and we appreciate that. You're free to leave if you wish."

Gideon noticed the man's Adam's apple bob a couple of times as if he was deeply moved by her words.

He licked his lips before speaking. "Thank you. But if it had not been for your kindness when I staggered in here with a message from your son, then collapsed with fever, I probably wouldn't be alive. So thank you both, but my original plan to stay has not changed."

"Hurrah!" Gideon yelled happily.

His mother gave him a disapproving glance, but her eyes flickered to Fletcher. He grinned, his eyes bright. Mrs. Tugwell met his gaze; then slowly a smile crept across her face.

★ ★

★ ★ ★ ★ ★

Emily led a saddled horse toward her early morning meeting with Toombs. She saw his eyes harden and a dark scowl of displeasure settle over his face.

"What're you up to?" he demanded harshly.

"William's orders," she answered, trying to force a light tone. "He wants me to ride with you today, then tonight report what I have seen."

"Now, look!" the overseer rumbled, his mouth working with anger. "I put up with taking orders through you because you've been nice to me, even if you are just a slip of a girl and a Yankee at that."

Emily grimaced at his belligerency and personal slur, but she waited, having expected an eruption.

Toombs rushed on. "But I will not have you riding through the tobacco and disturbing the field hands! You go tell your cousin that either he leaves me alone to run this place, or he can get himself another overseer!"

Emily didn't know if it was a bluff or not, but she had no intention of backing down. In another month, she would be on her way home to Illinois. She could put up with the temperamental overseer until then.

"I'll tell him," she said politely. "But not until I've finished my ride with you."

"I told you that you're not riding with me!"

"Then I shall follow you. Is that what you want?"

He sputtered, his face livid. Then he tried to stare her down. She locked her eyes with his and refused to blink or look away. After a few seconds when she thought he understood she meant what she said, she smiled.

"Mr. Toombs, in another month, I'll be out of your life forever. Meanwhile, we've got a job to do, so let's do it in the same manner we have so far."

He puffed up as if he were about to explode, but it was obvious he could not change the situation.

She moved quickly to add something she had thought about

★ ★

when watching Toombs' children playing with the little slaves. "If we agree on this, I'd like to do something for your children."

"*My* children?" He sounded genuinely surprised.

"Yes, I know you want them to have the very best lives they can have, including education. The school's been closed for more than a year. With your permission, while I'm here, I'd like to give your younger children a start on how to read and write. You'd like them to know how to do that, wouldn't you?"

Toombs stared at her in silence for a few seconds. Then he relaxed. "You're the sauciest female I ever met," he complained with a hint of a smile. "But all right. Mount up! Let's ride and talk about our deal."

★ ★ ★ ★ ★

The next two weeks were about the happiest ones that Gideon had known since his father died. Although very tired, he rode to Briarstone every Monday, Wednesday, and Friday evening. Each time, before starting the session, Emily reported on her teaching of the Toombs children.

After the first few lessons given the younger ones, the father had asked her if his older ones could also attend. She agreed, and even the two boys in their teens came after first protesting. However, they soon fell under Emily's spell of sincere, warm attention and tutoring.

Gideon showed up the second Monday in August to find Emily sitting glumly on the top front step at Briarstone.

"Something the matter?" he asked, forgetting his weariness and hurrying toward her in the gathering dusk.

"I got a couple of letters today," she said, looking up at him with sadness in her violet eyes.

"Bad news?" he guessed.

"Yes and no." She turned toward the massive front door, which stood open. "Julie! Gideon's here!" Emily turned back to face Gideon, who sat down beside her.

"She's been up talking with her brother because Uncle George just brought the mail a short time ago. He received news about Nat."

★ ★

Gideon's thoughts shifted to long ago, recalling when Nat had secretly helped him learn to read in a "pit school." Just a few weeks ago, Emily and Gideon had briefly visited with Nat in Richmond.

"What's happened to him?"

"William got word that Nat's been captured south of Richmond and is being held at a small plantation."

Gideon mused, "If William gets him back . . ."

"I know," Emily finished. "As soon as William is able, he'll whip him to within an inch of his life, then sell him into the Deep South so he can never escape."

"I am so sorry," Gideon whispered. "Really sorry."

"Me too. But that's not the only news. I got a letter from Brice."

This upset Gideon, but he kept that out of his voice. "Are prisoners of war allowed to write letters?"

"I guess so. He said Mrs. Stonum gave him this address. His wounded arm is healing, but he's still weak. Once, when I was helping at the hospital in Richmond, he told me that he was going to escape. Mrs. Stonum said he was just trying to impress me."

Gideon controlled the resentment that roared through him. "I'm not surprised," he said coolly.

Emily sadly shook her head. "I got a second letter from Mrs. Stonum. She started out by saying she'll be here August twenty-fifth, and we'll leave for Illinois on the twenty-seventh."

Emily hesitated before adding, "She also said that Brice has escaped from Libby Prison!"

LESSONS, PAST
AND PRESENT

Gideon finished the chores early on Wednesday and arrived at Briarstone before dusk. He dismounted from the mule and started toward the front door when he heard William's angry voice from in back of the big house. A second, softer voice was Emily's.

Memories of when William had yelled at and then beat on him made Gideon want to mount up and leave. But he could not do that, and he no longer feared that he would receive another beating.

He walked around to where William sat in a rolling chair under a great tree. Levi, his personal body servant, stood silently behind him. Emily faced William while Julie sat in an outdoor chair with a stack of newspapers on her lap. From behind the English box hedges, Gideon was surprised to see several young slaves peering at the white people. Nobody noticed Gideon.

Emily bent so that her face was even with William's. She said quietly, "They were listening, and I saw no harm in teaching them how to write the first few letters of the alphabet."

"That's against the law!" William shouted, causing the black children to break away from the hedge and run toward the slave quarters. "You know that, Emily, so why do you aggravate me by doing such a thing?"

"I wasn't thinking about that," she replied. "I just thought of them as children interested in learning—"

"They're black, so they must remain illiterate!" William broke in. "That's the law! Do you understand?"

Emily took a slow breath before answering, "No, I really do not. I believe everyone, black or white, should be able to read and write. But I'll respect your wishes."

"Good!" William turned his head toward Levi. "Take me back in the house."

As the body slave started to obey, William caught sight of Gideon mutely watching from a discreet distance. William looked straight at him, but neither spoke nor raised a hand as he was wheeled up a ramp at the side of the house. It was a reminder that Gideon was tolerated but not really welcome at Briarstone.

Emily apologized as Gideon approached. "I'm sorry about that." She gave him a welcoming smile. "We've been getting along reasonably well. I had hoped to make these last couple of weeks go as smoothly before I leave."

Mentioning her going away gave Gideon a quick, sharp pain of regret, but he didn't know how to tell her how very important she had become in his life. He merely nodded and greeted Julie.

She stood up and handed him a newspaper. "Something must be up," she said, obviously changing the subject. "See for yourself."

He waited for Emily to sit beside Julie before he sat down and glanced at the front page. He read silently for several seconds, then looked at the girls. "I think you're right, Julie," he said, "something is up."

"Something big," Emily added. "General McClellan is evacuating Harrison's Landing and heading north toward Alexandria. That's just this side of the Potomac River and a few miles from Washington. William says McClellan must be going to help Pope against General Lee."

Something in her voice alerted Gideon to some concern she had. He asked, "Are you afraid that maybe they're preparing for a showdown between Lee and Pope?"

"That," she admitted with a slight tremor in her tone, "and that they might do so before Mrs. Stonum gets here and we can leave for the Union lines."

Julie explained, "If there's a big battle between here and the Potomac River, she may not be able to get through. Then she

★ ★

would have to stay here for the rest of the war, however long that lasts."

Gideon saw confirmation of that fear in Emily's eyes. He hesitated, torn between a personal wish that she stay and knowing her strong desire to go north. He tried to find the right words to comfort her.

"Remember in Sunday school," he began, "about Joseph in the Bible? He was about our age when his brothers sold him into slavery down in Egypt. Remember?"

"Of course," Emily replied. "Practically everyone, both North and South, knows all the Bible stories."

"Well, remember how years later Joseph had become second only to Pharaoh when his brothers came to Egypt to buy food because of a famine in their homeland? Joseph told them that God had turned what they did into something good. So maybe you should stay here and—"

"This isn't the same thing!" Emily broke in. "Not at all! I just want to get back to my home in Illinois."

"I hope you do," Gideon said sincerely. "But no matter what happens, remember that things will work out."

"You heard William a moment ago, Gideon!" Emily protested. "You know how difficult things were when I lived here before! Oh, we've gotten along fine so far, but he's starting to get well. When he is, then what?"

When Gideon didn't answer, Emily held up her newspaper. "All right, let's begin our lesson."

★　★　★　★　★

Since being captured and severely whipped by patrollers, Nat had been returned to Trumble's plantation, where he fought against discouragement. His mother's teachings still rang in his ears: *"Winning is in the mind, not the muscles."* But for the first time in his life, little worms of doubt wiggled into his thoughts.

Too much time had elapsed to ever expect to catch up to his brother, even if Nat could again escape. He knew that he should soon run away again because by now William would have received word to come and reclaim him.

Knowing that William would savagely whip him before selling him into the Deep South added to Nat's gloomy thoughts. He sat against the side of a ramshackle cabin and realized what all people of his color had known from birth: There was no hope, no future.

Yet around him the field hands were tending their small gardens or smoking their pipes and talking among themselves in the gathering dusk. The little boys were playing marbles and "Anty over," and racing on foot.

Some small girls were playing with corn-shuck dolls while others were gathered in a ring drawn in the dirt. They clapped hands, sang, and danced inside the circle. In one of the cabins, some women were singing spirituals and shouting. For the first time, Nat wished he had something that these people possessed. Their faith helped them to live on in hope of something better to come.

Nat was so preoccupied that he was not aware anyone was near until someone sat down beside him. He turned listless eyes to see Orpheus.

"I'm sorry you got caught," he said so quietly that Nat barely heard the words. "I hope your hands are healing, although I don't see how that could be since they put you in the fields all day."

Nat didn't feel like talking, so he said nothing.

Orpheus glanced around to make sure nobody was close before he whispered, "Remember that barn I showed you one Sunday when we were walking to church?"

Nat recalled the barn, which was said to belong to an abolitionist, and he nodded.

Orpheus leaned closer. "You heard about conductors?"

Nat stirred at the word. "Yes. Why?"

"That conductor is getting ready to ship some packages north by boat." Orpheus cocked his head to look closely at Nat, obviously meaning for him to understand what he meant but would not dare speak aloud.

It might have been a trap, but Nat didn't care much. What fate could be worse than what he knew faced him? "So?" he asked under his breath.

"Packages have to be in the barn in the next few days." Orpheus paused, then added, "Can't be late."

Nat studied the other slave and believed him. "Thanks, Orpheus," he whispered. "I'll remember."

Orpheus dreamed of freedom but was afraid to try, Nat reminded himself. But Nat would keep trying.

★　★　★　★　★

Gideon carried the slop bucket of kitchen scraps to the pigpen, where Fletcher stood outside watching the big black boar.

"He's going to be a prime hog when butchering time comes around," Fletcher commented.

"Can't be too soon for me," Gideon replied, shifting the heavy mixture of milk, vegetable parts, and old biscuits to his other hand. "Get him to follow you to the shed while I pour this into his trough."

Fletcher had already started walking along the fence toward the closed-in shelter. The boar followed, grunting a warning and thrusting his snout against the rails. When man and hog reached the shed at the far end of the pen, Gideon quickly stood on the bottom rail, lifted the pail, and hastily poured the contents into the wooden trough. Instantly, the animal ran toward it, squealing.

Gideon jumped down and backed up to watch the hog noisily eating. It would be good to have the dangerous animal turned into human food, but when that happened, Fletcher would be back in the Shenandoah. Gideon's mother would not be humming a hymn, as he could hear her doing now through the open kitchen window.

Fletcher walked up to Gideon. "Has your friend Emily heard any more about her escaped Yankee soldier?"

"Not a word, the last I knew," Gideon replied. "But I figure he's had enough time to sneak across the Potomac into Union lines. That is, unless he found some of his own Yankees, or maybe our troops have caught him."

"Any of those are possible, I suppose." Fletcher turned away from the hogpen and looked around the Tugwell farm. "This sure is a mighty fine little place."

Gideon glanced sharply at the man, hoping that he was having

★　★

second thoughts about moving away in the fall. "I like it," Gideon replied, "although I don't like the work. Someday, when the war is over and Isham returns, I'll gladly leave it and go to Richmond to be a writer."

Gideon hesitated, thinking how to phrase the thought that leaped to his mind. "Of course, I could maybe go sooner if someone else took over here."

Fletcher gave no indication that he understood the not-too-subtle meaning in the boy's words. "If this war drags on, you may be old enough to have to go off and fight the Yankees yourself."

"Ah, the war won't last that long."

"I hope not. But at church last Sunday, I read a couple of newspapers that someone had left on his buggy seat. I figured he wouldn't mind."

Gideon recalled what Julie said about something being up, and what the paper reported about McClellan moving away from the peninsula toward Alexandria. He asked Fletcher, "You think something's going to happen?"

"No doubt." Fletcher looked toward Briarstone. "I hope Emily gets across the Potomac before then."

"What do you think will happen?"

"I'm guessing, of course, but General Lee and General Jackson are men who like to take the offensive, to attack. Lee did that at Richmond against great odds and made McClellan retreat. In the Shenandoah, Jackson outsmarted and outfought six Union armies with a lot more men than he had. I suspect Lee and Jackson are about to attack again."

Alarm seized Gideon. "Attack? Where?"

"I don't know, but I have an idea. I was with your brother Isham at Manassas a year ago in July. That was good ground for a pitched battle then; could be again."

"But Manassas is between here and the Potomac!" Gideon exclaimed. "If that happens before Emily gets to the river . . ." He left his thought unfinished.

"Let's hope it takes all those men so much time to get ready that Emily's safely in the North before then."

Gideon started to nod but stopped himself, again torn between

★ ★

his wanting her to stay and knowing how very much she wanted to get back to Illinois.

Fletcher broke into his musings. "One good thing for us right now is that we don't have to worry about Cobb sneaking around here for a while."

"Oh?" Gideon's eyes shot up. "How so?"

"I heard that William sent him to bring back his runaway body servant."

Gideon closed his eyes as if he had been hit in the stomach, fearing what the slave catcher would do to Nat.

★ ★ ★ ★ ★

The August heat and humidity was oppressive as Emily made her daily horseback ride through the tobacco fields that spread out around Briarstone's three-story house. Black men and women, with children as young as nine or ten, labored in the wide-leafed plants under a burning sun. Emily glanced at the sky, hoping the gathering clouds would soon provide shade, if not rain.

She had charmed Toombs by listening attentively and avoiding any possible controversy. Since William had sent her to make daily on-site inspections, Toombs had told her about planting the seed, hoeing, weeding, and removing suckers. She had been repulsed by hearing how the big green worms as round as a finger had to be picked off by hand and killed. Now the leaves were turning yellow, indicating prime time for picking, and the field hands bent over the plants while Emily and Toombs rode along the rows.

"So," he said as if finishing a thought, "what do you think?"

Emily was stumped. Her mind had drifted to her main concern: having Mrs. Stonum arrive so they could leave for the Union lines. Originally, her principal interest had been in getting across the Potomac before the time limit on their passes had expired. Now, recalling the last few weeks of newspaper reports, she had a newer, more immediate apprehension about opposing armies moving between her and home.

She tried to force herself to recall what she must have subconsciously heard the overseer say, but it was a vain effort. Finally

★ ★

she confessed, "I'm sorry. My mind sort of wandered off."

"It's no wonder, with all this heat and humidity. Now, if you was a boy, I'd say you should ride to the end of this row with me, then slip on down to the river and jump in. It'd be nice and cool."

Emily smiled. "My brothers used to do that, but a girl doesn't have such freedom."

"I suppose not, although I doubt anyone would see you down in the river bottom. You could dip your wrists in the water and maybe splash some on your face."

Anxious to get away before he returned to whatever point he had been trying to make, she nodded. "I believe I will do exactly that." She turned her horse's head down the row and lightly touched her heels to his flanks. "I'll catch up with you in a little while," she added.

"Watch out for water moccasins," he called after her as she rode away.

The gathering summer storm clouds cut off the sun before she reached the canopy of trees along the river. It was quiet except for the drumming of a woodpecker on a dead snag and the distant call of a bobwhite hidden in the underbrush. She glanced around apprehensively, first at the sky now rumbling with approaching thunder, then at the ground along the river, where a poisonous cottonmouth might be nearly invisible. She wished Julie was with her, or at least that it wasn't such a lonely place.

She heard a voice and reined in sharply, her eyes probing the direction from which the sound had come. Then she sighed with relief. *It's Gideon giving orders to his mule!* They were across the Briarstone/Tugwell snake fence that marked the boundary, but too far away to call. Gideon loaded some downed limbs onto a sledge, unaware of her.

She realized with a pang of regret that she would miss him when she returned to Illinois. But that was life: People met, people parted. Life went on anyway.

She eased from the saddle and tied the reins loosely to the lower branch of a tree. Cautiously, watching her step, she made her way down a slanted embankment. She looked toward Gideon, but he was no longer in sight. She glanced back toward the river

★ ★

just as a turtle slid off a log jutting out over the small stream.

She began loosening the cuffs on her long sleeves in anticipation of thrusting her wrists into the cool water. She stepped around a tangle of berry vines and stopped dead still. A man's well-worn boot stuck out from under some low-growing brush. For a second, she thought it was an abandoned boot. Then she saw a leg covered by the brush. The leg moved!

She involuntarily sucked in her breath and stepped back. Her heart leaped into a wild gallop as she turned to run toward her horse.

A weak voice called out, "Wait! Emily, wait!"

★ ★

AN ESCAPED YANKEE
PRISONER OF WAR

A shadow cast by a cloud made Nat look up from where he bent over in Trumble's tobacco rows within sight of the wide expanse of the James River. Nat stretched in a vain effort to ease his aching back muscles. This brought a warning shout from the black slave driver who set the pace that all other field hands had to match.

Nat had been unable to keep up, but neither the driver nor the white overseer whipped him: The reward might be less if a runaway slave was unable to work when his owner or his representative came to reclaim "property."

A girl about seven or eight staggered across the field with a heavy wooden bucket containing water for the workers. Nat started to motion for her to bring him a drink, but his hand stopped abruptly in midair.

A white man on a mule had ridden up to the overseer at the far end of the row. Nat stared. *Barley Cobb! William must have sent him for me!*

Nat saw the overseer point toward him with the whip he always carried. Cobb shaded his eyes as the sun emerged from behind a cloud. Nat turned and ran through the tobacco plants and past startled field hands. A yell from both Cobb and the overseer spurred Nat on. He dashed toward the James River, fear driving him to escape, even if he had little chance of outrunning a mounted man.

* * * * *

Lightning in the distance danced across the darkening sky as Gideon hurried to load the last limb onto the sledge. He wanted to get home before the storm struck. He picked up the reins and called, "Git up" to the mule. As the thunder rumbled ominously toward him, he heard his name shouted from the Briarstone property.

Startled, he looked in the direction of the call and saw a girl with golden hair running toward him in the river bottom. He sucked in his breath in recognition. "Emily! What's she doing?"

"Gideon! Gideon!" Her frightened voice shattered his question. Holding up her long skirt with one hand to run better, she frantically waved the other. "I need help!"

Quickly throwing the end of the reins around a low bush, Gideon sprinted toward her as fast as his heavy work brogans would permit. Wild thoughts raced through his mind.

Maybe she's being chased. No, there's nobody behind her! Maybe Julie got hurt, or maybe Emily got snakebit!

They arrived at the boundary fence together. Emily panted, "He's sick!" She pointed behind her. "Very sick!"

"Who?" Gideon asked, looking the way she pointed but without seeing anybody.

"Brice! I found him—"

"Brice?" Gideon interrupted in disbelief. "He's here?"

"Yes! He's burning up with fever, but he babbled something. I didn't understand all of it before he passed out. But I know he's got to have help or he'll die!"

Gideon hesitated, his mind spinning like a tornado. He had never really liked Brice, mostly because he said he intended to marry Emily when she grew up. But Brice was also an escaped Yankee prisoner of war.

"Please!" Emily broke into Gideon's thoughts. "Help me think what to do!"

Forcing all other distractions from his mind, Gideon focused on how to do that. "Take me to him," he said. "Then we can decide what to do."

"Thank you!" Turning away and again lifting her long skirts

★ ★

above her shoe tops, Emily started back through the trees. "Please hurry!"

"I am," Gideon replied and ran alongside her toward the river. A terrifying thought hit him: *Emily's a Yankee, so it's all right for her to help a Union soldier. But if I help, isn't that a crime against the Confederacy? Could I be hanged for that?*

★　★　★　★　★

Many miles away, Nat staggered wearily across the last stretch of green grass and into a grove of trees. Without a plan, he had run this way in a wild flight to escape Cobb's brutal hands. Nat had managed to elude his pursuer and his mule during a race through tangled vines and low-growing brush.

But Nat didn't think that Cobb would quit, even if he did not have any hounds with him. He might borrow some. So Nat kept moving, reeling with exhaustion and the aches of his field work, seeking the one possible place that might offer him a chance to escape.

He took heart when he smelled the James River. He took hope from the special fragrance of dense brush and trees that grew along its banks. Straining to see through the stand of trees, Nat caught glimpses of the water. Even under a glowering sky, it offered hope.

The river was far too wide to swim even if Nat knew how. It seemed to cut off further flight, but he wobbled on toward it, knowing that if hounds were loosed on his trail, they could not follow him in water. If he did not drown, he might either wade or pull himself along the bank by overhanging vines or exposed tree roots.

His breathing was so irregular and labored that he was almost sobbing as he hungrily gulped in air, then stopped at the riverbank and looked back. There was no sign of Cobb, but that was not a great reassurance. Nat swung back to look at the water stretching a mile or so into the distance. It was another discouraging sight.

Gunboats flying Union flags moved slowly on the wide surface. Various small craft hugged the far shore. A small river steamer a couple hundred feet off the near shore trailed smoke as it beat its way upriver toward Richmond.

Orpheus's words leaped into Nat's mind. He could not recall the exact words, but he remembered the basics: A "conductor" on the secret Underground Railroad was getting some fugitive slaves ready to ship north by boat. Those were to meet in the abolitionist's barn that Orpheus had pointed out to Nat one day on the way to church.

But when? Nat asked himself as he gingerly eased into what he hoped was shallow water. *The next few days; that's all I remember. Except they must not be late.*

The James was colder than Nat expected, making him take a sudden, sharp breath that seemed to collide with his rapid exhaling from the hard run. He held on to some overhanging willow branches and gingerly eased his feet down until he touched bottom. Slowly, he sank until only his head was above the surface. Then, ignoring all else, he began pulling himself downstream under the overhanging willows and other brush.

I can't find Rufus now, he sadly admitted, *but at least I'm still free. If I can get to that barn, maybe I can still find him someday; maybe my little brothers, also.*

The hope that had frayed like a weakening rope now seemed to be strengthened. *I've got to try. . . .*

A mule brayed, making Nat lift his head to see above the bank. Cobb was riding straight toward him. In spite of his breathing still not being quite normal, Nat took a deep breath and forced his head under the surface.

★ ★ ★ ★ ★

It made Gideon concerned that he was trespassing on William's property, but that was nothing compared to the troubled thoughts he experienced when he knelt to examine Brice.

Emily said, "He recognized me. When I first looked at him, he smiled just like he did when he used to tease his sister and me back home in Illinois. He muttered something about getting home, then passed out."

Emily had soaked her small, dainty handkerchief in the water

★ ★

and laid it across Brice's fevered brow. He had obviously exchanged his prisoner-of-war clothing for some ill-fitting men's
trousers, shirt, and boots.

"He needs a doctor," Gideon said. "But even if we can get ol'
Doc Janssen to come out, he would have to tell the sheriff or
somebody. Besides, I think maybe it's treason to help a Yankee
soldier, even if he is sick."

"But he's my friend! I can't just leave him here!"

"I know." Gideon glanced toward Briarstone's solid-looking
three-story house. There would be no help for a Yankee there.
William would have him turned over to the authorities immediately. Gideon's eyes darted to where his family's house was hidden
in the trees. Fletcher had lost a hand to Yankees. He would not
want to help Brice.

Not that I want to, either, Gideon told himself, *but I've got to
do something so he won't die.*

Turning back to Emily, Gideon gently took her by both hands.
They were trembling. He told her, "I'll go talk to my mother. Can
you wait here until I come back?"

She frowned, then shook her head. "I've got to get back because the overseer could come looking for me and might find
Brice. But maybe I can get some food from the kitchen. . . . No,"
she stopped herself, "he's too sick to eat. But he'll need drinking
water. I'll get some and meet you back here as soon as possible."

"Be careful," Gideon urged, wondering what he was getting
himself into. A streak of lightning directly overhead was instantly
followed by an ominous crash of thunder. Gideon flinched and
started running back toward Hercules as the storm burst in all
its fury.

★　★　★　★　★

Satisfied that Cobb had temporarily given up hunting him,
Nat crawled out of the James River well down from where he had
entered it. He was more afraid of Cobb than the jagged streaks of
lightning. The rain didn't bother him after his immersion in the
river, but failure to rescue his brother nagged him. He shook his

head, driving away the discouraging thought to focus on his situation.

Cobb may be back with dogs, Nat reminded himself. *They can follow my trail to where I went in, but they'll lose time finding where I came out. If I can get a ride so they can't track me, and can reach that abolitionist's barn in time, maybe I can—*

He broke off his contemplation at the sound of a team plodding along the dirt road a hundred yards away. Through the trees, Nat saw that the wagon driver was black. Sloshing in his shoes, Nat ran to intercept him.

★ ★ ★ ★ ★

Soaked to the skin, Gideon stood on the front of the sledge ahead of the load of limbs and hurried the mule into the barn. He heard his little brother and sisters playing in the haymow.

Gideon glanced toward the corner where Fletcher had his living quarters. *I hope the rain's driven him in there*, Gideon thought as he jumped off the sledge. *I won't tell anyone except Mama*, he told himself. *There's no sense in anyone else knowing about Brice, especially Mr. Fletcher.*

With head down against the pelting rain, Gideon sprinted across the bare ground now smelling of the rain. He bounded up the two short steps onto the covered back porch and stopped at the sight of his mother and Fletcher. He had obviously taken refuge from the storm.

Thinking quickly, Gideon said, "Mama, I need to talk to you in the kitchen."

She took one look at his agitated face and reached for the doorknob. "Please excuse us, John."

Gideon followed her inside, then quickly closed the door and leaned against it. "Mama!" he said in a hoarse whisper, "Emily's got trouble, and maybe I do, too!"

★ ★ ★ ★ ★

After making an excuse to Toombs, Emily rapidly rode through the rain to the big house. She tried to figure out how to take water back to Brice without arousing suspicion. But when

★ ★

she dismounted at the well, Julie came out of the house.

She called, "Emily, what're you doing over there?"

Emily didn't want to tell anyone about finding Brice—not even Julie. Hesitating, Emily raised her voice. "I . . . I want some water fresh from the well."

"You're sopping wet! Come in out of the rain and let the servants draw water for you."

"Thanks, but I'd rather do it myself." Emily turned to reach for the chain and bucket suspended over the well.

"Is something wrong?" Julie called.

"It's all right. I'm fine." Emily tried to sound calm and confident, but she heard the door close. She looked around and groaned at the sight of Julie hurrying toward her, using her open palm to shield her face from the raindrops.

"What is it?" Julie asked, drawing near.

"I . . ." Emily began, then stopped, unable to lie. "Please don't ask any questions. Just go back inside."

"Something *is* wrong!" Julie declared in alarm. "Tell me!"

"No!" Emily spoke more firmly than she intended, then finished in a whisper, "I don't want you involved!"

"Involved in what?"

Emily whispered fervently, "Believe me, Julie, you don't want to know!"

"Yes, I do! We're friends! You can trust me!"

Emily believed that but still didn't want Julie to risk getting in trouble. Emily closed her eyes, thinking.

"Are you ill?" Julie demanded anxiously.

"No." Emily opened her eyes. "I'm fine, but if I do tell you, will you promise not to tell anyone else?"

"I promise! I promise! Now, what is it?"

Emily looked around to make sure nobody was close enough to overhear. Then she put her mouth close to Julie's ear and told her about Brice.

"What?" Julie cried, drawing back in shock.

"Shh! Keep your voice down!"

Julie whispered hoarsely, "What're you going to do?"

"First, I'm going to take him some water to drink. Then I've

★ ★

got to find some way to help him get well."

"You can't do that! He's an escaped Yankee prisoner of war! There are too many people at Briarstone to keep anything secret like that! You've got to turn him in!"

"Oh no! He's my friend! I couldn't do that!"

"Don't be ridiculous, Emily! Somebody will find out if you try to help him; then they'll take your passes away and you won't ever get back to Illinois!"

"My passes! I hadn't thought of that!"

"Well, now you have, and you're only a week from using them! So let's go tell my brother."

"No! Absolutely not! I thought about it on the ride back from the river. Brice must have realized that I'm the only person he knows in the South. That's why he came here! But the fever hit him before he could find a way to contact me privately. He trusts me, and I'm going to help him!"

"Even if you lose your passes, or worse?"

Emily sighed heavily. "Yes."

Julie vigorously shook her head. "I couldn't do that, but— well, if that's your decision, and you insist, I'll help you. So what are we going to do now?"

Emily swallowed hard. "I don't know yet, but let's go give him some water while I try to think."

★　★　★　★　★

After Gideon had finished his report about Brice, his mother whispered, "Isn't he one of those Yankee horsemen who caught Isham last year and then let him escape when they found out he was Emily's friend?"

"Well, Isham didn't say for sure that Brice had let him get away, but he sure made it possible."

"So if it weren't for Brice," Mrs. Tugwell mused, "Isham could be dying in a Yankee prisoner-of-war camp."

"I guess so, Mama."

"Let me think." She dropped heavily into her old hickory chair and began to vigorously rock. "You are already involved, so even if I help Brice, you're old enough that we both might be charged

★　★

with what's called 'aiding and abetting the enemy.' "

"Is that the same as treason, Mama?"

"I don't know. Barley Cobb would surely say so, but I wonder what John Fletcher thinks?"

"Do we have to tell him?"

"Yes, because I trust him. When he showed up here so sick he fainted, we put him in your and Ben's room, where I could treat him until he was well enough to move to the barn. But we can't do the same with Brice because of your little brother and sisters. They might let it slip and tell someone at the village store or church."

"So we're going to help Brice?"

"I have a moral obligation because of what he did for your stepbrother. Besides, in wartime, everyone makes sacrifices. I would not leave a sick dog out there in the rain, much less a boy made in God's image. Come on. We'll tell Mr. Fletcher and see if his conscience will let him help us save that boy's life."

TREASON OR COMPASSION?

John Fletcher raised both eyebrows and pursed his lips as Martha Tugwell quickly explained the situation, but he didn't speak.

She finished by saying, "Yankee or not, that sick boy is one of God's children. I know it's asking a lot for you to help. I don't want you to do it against your conscience, but I have to ask how you feel about this."

Lightning crackled overhead and thunder instantly boomed as Fletcher silently looked down at Mrs. Tugwell. Gideon saw his jaw muscles twitch when he slowly turned and looked thoughtfully into the rain.

"Martha," he began, speaking slowly and softly, "I am more grateful than I can say because you took me in when I was a sick stranger and nursed me back to health. I owe you my life."

"Wait a minute!" she said quickly. "I told you before; you owe us nothing. We only did our duty. I don't want you to feel obligated to help us because of that!"

"Martha," Fletcher said, turning back to face her, "I hate Yankees! Oh, I know it's not right to hate, but I lost my wife and son to them! I lost my farm, my hand . . ." His voice broke and he fell silent.

"I know," Mrs. Tugwell said so softly that Gideon barely heard her. "I understand, and I can't blame you. Please forgive me for even mentioning that boy." She took a step as if to leave the shelter of the porch.

"Wait!" Fletcher said firmly. "Think what this means! It might be considered treason—betraying a promise to protect the Confederacy against her enemy."

"Mr. Fletcher," she said coolly, "that's a boy out there, too sick to be an enemy! I respect your right to think differently! So I'm sorry I bothered you. Now all I'm asking is that you not tell anyone about this. Is that too much to ask?"

"No, Mrs. Tugwell," Fletcher replied frostily. "It's not too much. You have my word: I'll not tell anyone."

Gideon sensed the tension between them made them switch from using their first names to the formal surnames.

Gideon's mother said bruskly, "Thank you, Mr. Fletcher! Please bring the children inside the house and keep them away from the windows when we return." She glanced at Gideon and stepped into the rain. "Let's take the mule and go get that boy."

Gideon followed, surprised and distressed at the unexpected quarrel between his mother and Fletcher.

Does this mean the end of my hopes that Mama will ever be happy again? What will happen if Cobb or someone finds out about us aiding an escaped Yankee prisoner?

★   ★   ★   ★   ★

Nat was grateful that the black driver let him ride in the farm wagon without making conversation. By then, the rain had drenched them both so that Nat's unplanned dip in the James River wasn't as obvious as it might have been. There was comfort in the fact that the downpour had probably erased Nat's footprints where he had climbed into the wagon. Even if Cobb returned with hounds, there would be neither scent nor tracks to show which way Nat had gone.

They were heading toward the Trumble plantation. There was danger in that, but Nat had no choice if he wanted to reach the abolitionist's barn. Near there, Nat planned to leave the wagon and walk away from the barn so as to mislead the driver in case patrollers or Cobb questioned him later. Nat glanced over his shoulder as the road turned to mud, slowing team and wagon. But when he turned around after a second look back, he noticed that the driver seemed nervous. To avoid making him too suspicious,

Nat didn't look back again. He silently hunched down against the rain as the team neared the white man's church where Nat had walked to services. *It won't be long now*, he told himself, *but I hate to leave without Rufus.*

★ ★ ★ ★ ★

Emily and Julie found that the precipitation on Brice's face had roused him from his unconsciousness. He had managed to sit up in the brush and cup his hands to catch the fresh rainwater to ease his fevered throat. After introducing her cousin, Emily explained the situation.

"We can't take you to the big house where we live," she began, brushing raindrops from her forehead. "There are too many people around, so it would be impossible to hide you. I'm sorry, but the best Julie and I can do is bring an India-rubber blanket or some canvas to spread over this brush to help keep you dry."

Emily wasn't sure that he understood her, although he looked at her with fevered eyes that somehow did not seem to really focus.

Julie added quickly, "We'll bring you food and fresh water, and we'll come as often as we can, but—" She broke off abruptly. "What's that?"

The girls both stood up and listened, trying to peer through the downpour and hear between thunder peals.

Emily caught a movement in the trees nearest the river where the boundary fence ended. Her pulse speeded up; then she laughed with relief. "It's Gideon with his mother and their mule!"

Emily stepped out of the brush where he could see her. She smiled and waved at him.

Gideon stood at the front of the sledge. He released one hand from the reins and waved back at Emily, but he did not smile. The thunder rumbled into the distance, heralding the end of the storm. He eased Hercules around the last post and entered Briarstone property. That was something he rarely did, and each time he became anxious. But instead of William watching him, he saw Emily, Julie, and Brice. Gideon frowned at the sight of the Yankee.

★ ★

"Remember," his mother said from behind him, "do this as fast as possible with a minimum of talk. Then we'll get him back to our place and hide him, as we discussed on the way over here. Are we still agreed?"

"Yes, Mama." He turned the mule away from the river, hearing the sledge runners sliding over the lush grass on Briarstone property. It was a pleasant sound, but Gideon was too concerned about what could happen. He barely noticed as Hercules plodded toward the girls and Brice.

I don't like this, Gideon told himself, *for there's no way it can turn out to be anything but big trouble!*

★ ★ ★ ★ ★

After the black teamster stopped at the edge of the muddy road, Nat jumped as far as possible from the wagon into the roadside grass. He wanted to avoid leaving his footprints in the mud. He suspected that the driver knew he was a runaway, but there had been no indication that Nat would be betrayed.

Still, to be safe, Nat deliberately walked off into the woods at an angle. This took him away from the barn, but he was still on the same side of the road so that he would not leave any scent or tracks by crossing it.

After several minutes the rain eased, then stopped. Nat carefully circled back and approached the barn from the backside. He protected himself as much as possible by hiding behind a tree. Only part of his head showed as he peeked around the trunk to study the barn.

It was strangely quiet, making Nat uneasy. Were there really some fugitive slaves waiting for the final ride to the river steamer that was supposedly going to take them north to freedom? Or was the barn a trap where white patrollers were waiting to grab him?

Nat decided to delay until dark to cross the last open space where he might be seen. He started to ease down the tree trunk to a sitting position when he caught a flash of movement at the edge of the woods several yards away.

A black boy in rags nervously stepped into the open, glanced wildly around, then sprinted toward the barn. Nat sucked in his

★ ★

breath, unable to believe what he saw.

"Rufus!" he exclaimed aloud.

★ ★ ★ ★ ★

Returning to the Tugwell farm, with his mother trying to comfort Brice in the middle of the sledge, Gideon fretted about its telltale runner tracks.

William likely won't see them, Gideon told himself in a vain attempt to ease his fears, *but if Cobb sneaks around and finds them, he'll follow them back to where the girls found Brice, and then to here. Cobb may tell William, or more likely, Cobb will bring the rangers down on us as he's threatened. It's all Brice's fault for coming here to see Emily! Why didn't he just head north out of Richmond and slip into some Union lines?*

In that moment, Gideon came close to hating Brice. But that thought shamed Gideon, so he violently shook his head and pulled back on the reins. The sledge stopped inside the barn.

Gideon turned to his mother sitting beside Brice, who lay on the sledge. "Let's get this done before Ben or one of the girls comes running out and sees what we're doing!"

★ ★ ★ ★ ★

In their wet garments, Emily and Julie slipped into the big house by a side door and hurried up the back stairs. They entered Julie's room because she had more changes of clothes than Emily.

Toby, Julie's young personal maid with the honey-colored skin, hurried in to help. She was accompanied by Lizzie, an attractive octoroon—a person with one-eighth African ancestry. Emily was uncomfortable with having a maid assigned to her, so she dismissed Lizzie. Julie did the same with Toby so the cousins could talk while they changed into dry clothes.

"I'm frightened," Julie confessed, dabbing at her hair with a towel. "If William finds out—"

"I know!" Emily interrupted, stripping down to her chemise. "But we couldn't leave him out there to die!"

"Well, I hope Gideon's mother is right and his fever is about to break. The sooner he leaves, the better."

★ ★

"I'm more concerned for Gideon and his family," Emily admitted. "They don't even know Brice, and yet they're risking an awful lot, and all because of me."

"I've been thinking on what Brice said about the reason he came here instead of just going north from Richmond. I know he's right about our troops being all over that area after General Lee and Stonewall Jackson drove the Yankees back from Richmond. But I think the real reason Brice came here was to see you."

"Really?" Emily asked.

"Really," Julie assured her. "I remember you telling me that he's said a couple of times he plans to marry you when you get older."

Emily said, "I shouldn't have told you that."

"Why not? We're friends. But did you tell Gideon?"

"Yes, because he's also a friend."

"You haven't noticed the way he looks at you since you got back from Richmond, or the look on his face when he was helping get Brice onto that sled."

Emily's eyebrows shot up. "No, I didn't, but what did you see?"

Julie shrugged. "I think Gideon considers you more than just a friend. He's going to be fourteen this fall, so I think—" She broke off suddenly, tiptoed to the door, and yanked it open.

Emily caught a glimpse of Toby hurrying down the hallway.

Julie closed the door and looked at Emily with wide, frightened eyes. "I think she was eavesdropping! If she tells my brother . . ." She left the words dangling.

Emily didn't answer, but she was filled with sudden fear.

★ ★ ★ ★ ★

Nat peered through a knothole in the back of the barn and saw a white man in a black slouch hat talking to a black boy in rags. Nat's heart leaped with delight when he took a closer look and confirmed that the boy was his younger brother Rufus. Many questions sprang to Nat's mind: *How did he get free from the coffle chain? What's he doing here? Is that man an abolitionist, or is he going to turn Rufus over to patrollers?*

★ ★

A tremendous desire to rush in and hug his brother almost overwhelmed Nat, but he hesitated, his eye still at the knothole. The man, dressed like a farmer, motioned up to a loft. Rufus nodded, ran to a rough ladder built against a beam, and rapidly climbed up. He burrowed out of sight under some sacks, and the farmer left the barn.

Nat eagerly watched him walk the hundred yards to his house and enter the back door. Then, barely able to contain his excitement, Nat silently slipped into the barn and hurried to the bottom of the ladder.

Looking up, he called softly, "Rufus! It's Nat!"

There was no answer, which didn't surprise Nat. He reached for the bottom rung of the ladder, calling in a hoarse whisper, "It's your brother! I'm coming up!"

Rufus still had given no sign of acknowledgment when Nat stood on the loft flooring and looked down at the pile of sacks. It was only when Nat gently lifted them that the white of his brother's frightened eyes showed. With a glad cry of recognition, Rufus leaped up. The brothers fell into each other's arms.

★　★　★　★　★

Gideon hurried to close the barn door, hoping Ben, Kate, and Lilly hadn't seen Brice lying face-up on the sledge. Fletcher stepped out on the back porch and hurried across the muddy ground. Gideon's brother and sisters instantly peered out the kitchen window.

Fletcher entered the barn as Gideon returned to help his mother off the sledge.

"Martha," Fletcher said quickly, "I'm ashamed of the way I acted a while ago. If you'll forgive me, I want to help with him." He jerked his chin toward Brice.

Her somber face lighted up with a relieved smile. "Do you realize that puts you at great risk, John?"

"I've faced worse. Now, he'll need care that you can't give him without the children finding out. So put him in my quarters, then keep them away. Gideon, please help me get him on his feet."

Gideon and Fletcher each put one of Brice's arms over their

★　★

shoulders and helped him walk on sagging legs to the far end of the barn. In the small area that had been built as Fletcher's quarters, they eased Brice on to the pole bunk bed, then walked out and closed the door.

The adults whispered something to each other, but Gideon didn't listen. He felt sorry for Brice, yet he didn't like anyone paying attention to Emily—especially an escaped Yankee prisoner of war. It wasn't just because he was an enemy soldier, but because of other dangers.

If Brice was discovered, Fletcher would undoubtedly be charged with treason. Maybe Gideon would, too. He wasn't sure what the authorities would do to his mother, but he was confident that there would be an effort to seize the Tugwell farm. Then what would happen to his little brother and sisters? It was a terrifying thought.

His mother broke into his reflections. "Did you see his horse? He said he left it near where we found him."

"No, but it must still be in the river bottom."

"You'd better go find it," she suggested. "Oh, while we were on our way here, Brice explained to me how he escaped and why he came here."

"I know why he came!" Gideon exclaimed. "He wanted to see Emily! He did that without any thought to what trouble it would cause her!" At once, Gideon regretted voicing his strong emotions against Brice.

"No, Gideon, he told me that he didn't plan to come this way at all," his mother replied. "But when he got sicker, he said that he was afraid he'd die unless he got help. Emily was the only person he knew in Virginia. As for how he escaped, he said that he caught fever in Libby Prison, so they transferred him to a hospital. The security there was not very tight, so even though he had fever, he got away, found a horse, and rode here. He said he'll go on toward the Potomac River as soon as possible. He doesn't want us or Emily to get in trouble."

Then he should have stayed away! Gideon thought, but he grudgingly admitted, "I suppose so."

He thought of the sledge tracks on Briarstone property—

★ ★

tracks that led directly to this barn. There was no way they could be erased except by time. But what if someone found them before then?

Especially Cobb! The idea jarred Gideon. *He's always hunting along the river, looking for signs of runaway slaves. I'm glad he's off somewhere. Maybe before he returns, Brice will be gone from here.*

Gideon's mother said she would return to the house to prepare her fever-reducing home remedy and fix something for Brice to eat. Fletcher walked with her.

Sighing, Gideon fearfully whispered to himself, "What have we gotten ourselves into?"

THE RANGERS
STRIKE

After Nat's and Rufus's first rush of excitement of finding each other in the abolitionist's barn loft, Nat asked how his brother had escaped from the coffle.

"Like most of us chained there," he replied in good English, which he had learned with Nat at their first master's place, "I had pretty much given up hope of ever being free. Then I saw you when that planter with the cane caught you. I watched him force you toward a house I thought must be his. I figured I'd find you there if I could get free, and then maybe we could escape together."

"I'm proud of you, Rufus, but what of the chains?"

"They were awful. We all had iron cuffs on one wrist. That cuff was attached to the long coffle chain. Once a day, the drovers released that wrist, made us step over the chain, then reattached the cuff to the other wrist, so we were back on the coffle chain. I guess they didn't want us to get sore wrists. We wouldn't be worth much if we couldn't work after walking clear to Georgia."

"I see!" Nat exclaimed. "I heard there was a secret to escaping the coffle, but I never learned what it was."

Rufus rushed on, the excitement in his voice still high. "There was also a short chain between my wrists, and that was attached to another chain around my waist. But one night when my wrist was out of the cuff, two of the men near the back end of the coffle got into a fight. While both drovers were breaking that up, I ran off and jumped into a creek by the road."

★ ★

"You can't swim, Rufus! You might have drowned!"

"I almost did, but I was so desperate I kept holding my breath, ducking under the water until the drovers gave up looking for me. Then I headed back this way. One night I found one of our people—a blacksmith—who cut off my chains. He told me about this barn. Tomorrow I was going to try to find out if you were still at that place where I saw you were headed that day."

Reality began to replace Nat's excitement. He motioned toward the house. "Who is that man?"

"He said, 'No names, please!' Then he went to get me something to eat. He'll soon take me and maybe some other what he called 'packages' to a small river steamer. Her captain is an abolitionist, like him. He'll take me aboard as his cabin boy and start me toward freedom. He said it wasn't wise to tell me any more. The less I knew, the better, in case I was caught again."

Nat smiled at his brother, who suddenly seemed to have drained away all his excited words. "If this farmer will include me in his 'packages,' we can go together. We should soon be safe in the North."

"I hope so, but I saw Duff, one of the drovers, riding along the public road a while ago. I'm sure he's looking for me."

"Same thing happened to me," Nat replied. "Trumble—the planter you saw catch me that day—must have sent word to my last owner, William Lodge. I was his body slave. I ran away from Trumble, and so far I've been able to escape from Barley Cobb. He's the man William sent to get me."

Nat hesitated before adding, "I hope Cobb finally gives up and goes away. However, with that drover looking for you, maybe we'd better not wait for the other 'packages' to arrive."

"But we don't know when or where the boat will dock."

Nat mused, "That's a problem, all right, unless . . ." he paused, thinking rapidly. From his own experiences, he knew that "conductors" usually took "packages" a short distance, mostly at night, then turned them over to another abolitionist who moved them to the next station. "Let's talk to the man who owns this barn," Nat said, "and see if he can start us toward freedom tonight!"

★ ★

★ ★ ★ ★ ★

On the next to last Saturday in August, Gideon hitched the mule to the wagon and drove his mother, Ben, and two younger sisters into the village of Church Creek. They needed supplies that the family couldn't grow or make themselves. Fletcher stayed home to make sure that Cobb didn't come poking around.

Going to town on Saturday was a rare treat for the family. Except for church, it was the only time they left the farm. Gideon tried to relax on the slow drive, but it was impossible to escape the tension over Brice still being hidden in the barn. Gideon had found his horse in the river bottom and tied it in the barn. Brice was still too weak to ride, although his fever had broken.

In the village, Gideon tied the mule under the shade of a large tree. Ben and the girls wanted to walk around, but their mother told them to stay in the wagon. They could talk to any friends who came by while their mother and Gideon shopped.

Gideon took the empty five-gallon coal-oil can and walked across the dusty street with his mother toward the small general store. There she wandered around, wistfully feeling fabric for clothes she couldn't afford before picking up a new glass chimney for a lamp.

Gideon automatically filled the can, then shoved a potato down over the spout as a cap and set it by the door. He idly wandered around the store, not consciously seeing anything because his thoughts were on Emily and Brice.

She planned to leave for the North next week, and that made Gideon unhappy. At the same time, he resented Brice even though Gideon knew it was wrong to do so. He was indignant that Brice had first put Emily in jeopardy by coming to her.

Gideon was still stewing inside when his mother finished her shopping. He carried her purchases in one hand and the coal-oil can in the other.

As they neared the wagon, Kate excitedly called to them. "Guess who we saw?"

Gideon was in no mood for guessing, but his mother asked, "Who?"

★ ★

"Barley Cobb!" Kate replied.

"Cobb?" Gideon turned to his mother. "I wonder when he got back? I hope he didn't catch Nat."

She didn't answer him but asked Kate, "What did Mr. Cobb want?"

"Nothing," she replied. "He was real nice. Said he had been over by the James River to pick up a runaway slave owned by William Lodge, but he had escaped again before he got there."

Mrs. Tugwell asked, "Is that all he talked about?"

"That's all," Kate replied. "Ask Ben and Lilly."

When Ben nodded, Gideon smiled in relief at his mother before he lifted the purchases over the tailgate. He turned to help her climb up into the wagon as five-year-old Lilly piped up.

"I told him we had a new horse in the barn, but we're not allowed to play there now."

"Oh," Gideon said a little uncertainly.

"Yes," Lilly continued, "and I told him that you and Mr. Fletcher sometimes take food to the hog on a plate instead of in the slop pail."

Gideon's heart lurched in alarm. He glanced at his mother and saw that her face had turned pale.

"Help me up!" she said quickly, then whispered, "Now we know for sure that Cobb's going to bring the rangers down on us! Let's get home and talk to Mr. Fletcher!"

★ ★ ★ ★ ★

Late August's afternoon heat and humidity forced Emily and Julie to hold their final Monday afternoon teaching session under the shade of an oak tree behind the big house. She had finished her lessons with the three youngest Toombs children and sent them to play with the slave children. She continued with teens Edwin and Wendell, and their twelve-year-old sister, Nancy.

Lacking books suitable for children with limited education, Emily substituted with the newspaper. "Julie," she said, handing it to her cousin, "skip the lead paragraph and just read the portion of President Lincoln's remarks inside the quotation marks."

Edwin grumbled from where he sat at the far end of the shade.

★ ★

"I don't care nothin' 'bout what he says. Read what Jeff Davis said."

Emily refused to be baited into a comment. She suspected that Edwin attended only to keep out of having to work and to look at her. She was uncomfortable with that, but she ignored his stares and remarks because both Wendell and Nancy were eager to learn.

Emily nodded to her cousin. "Go ahead, please."

" 'In great contests,' " Julie read aloud, " 'each party claims to act in accordance with the will of God, but one must be wrong. God cannot be for and against the same thing at the same time.' "

Edwin said, "That's easy. He's on our side."

Emily replied, "I expected you would say that. But do you think a Yankee would agree with you?"

"Yo're a Yankee," Edwin shot back. "So tell us."

She didn't answer when the geese began honking from the front of the big house. "Julie," she said, "could that be Mrs. Stonum? Her letter did say to expect her as early as today."

Edwin leaped up. "I'll go find out." He took a few steps to where he could see around the house, then turned back. A grin showed his crooked teeth. "It's your beau."

The word surprised Emily. "I don't have a beau."

"Well, Gideon would like to be."

"Gideon?" A slight frown creased Emily's brow. "He's not due for another couple of hours. Unless . . ." she didn't finish the thought. She exclaimed to the students, "That's all for today." She started hurrying toward the house, but Nancy and Wendell stopped her.

"Please don't go north with Mrs. Stonum!" Nancy pleaded, plucking uneasily at Emily's sleeve. "Me'n Wendell are learnin' real good, but if ye go away, we won't never get to read ner write."

"Don't go!" Wendell echoed, dropping his eyes and dragging a bare toe through the grass. "We need you!"

The request caught Emily by surprise, but she was distracted, worried about why Gideon had come so early. "We'll talk about it later," she said, then hurried off to meet Gideon.

The moment Emily saw his eyes, she knew something was wrong. She hurried up to him where he stood by the mule.

★ ★

"What is it?" she asked breathlessly.

He lowered his voice and repeated what Lilly had told Cobb in the village. Gideon concluded, "Since your friend sleeps in the same quarters as Mr. Fletcher, we figured that he would be safe enough these last couple of nights. But we're afraid Cobb will bring the rangers tonight, so we'll have to move him before then."

There was something about the way Gideon said "your friend" instead of using Brice's name that alerted Emily to some hidden feelings he had. "I'm sorry you got mixed up in this," she said softly. "I'll help, but I don't know what to do."

"You're leaving day after tomorrow, but we'll take care of him somehow."

"No!" She shook her head, making her long blond hair shimmer. "I can't leave until after he does!"

"But your passes!"

"They're good for about ten more days. I can wait."

"What'll you tell Mrs. Stonum and the others? And if you don't go, and General Lee's army meets Pope's between here and the Potomac? You may never get to Illinois!"

"You sound as if you want me to go," Emily said sadly.

"No, of course I don't! Uh . . ." he stumbled, aware that he had spoken from his feelings instead of his mind. He finished lamely, "I want you to do whatever you want."

"That's sweet, Gideon."

Her voice was so low that he barely heard. He looked up. "Here comes Julie. You going to tell her?"

"Maybe later. Come on, let's have our last lesson together, and maybe by the time it ends, we'll think of what should be done about . . . him."

Gideon nodded and followed her back around the house, keenly aware that they would soon have to say good-bye—maybe forever.

★　★　★　★　★

It was so dark inside the old warehouse that neither Nat nor his brother could see anything when night settled over the wharf area. The heat of the day lingered in their small, hidden room.

Night sounds replaced the dock ones: the screech of an owl, two cats fighting, and far in the distance, that same mysterious bugle melody heard from various camps on both sides of the river.

Most of the river noises were gone or muted, for it was risky running at night with lights that only cast a pale yellow beam a few feet. Overhead, Nat caught the tiny scratchings and squeaks of mice or rats in the rafters.

Then there came a footfall from outside the wall. Both boys were instantly alert. The steps approached slowly, cautiously. There was no flicker of a candle or lantern under the concealed door.

Rufus whispered, "Do you think it's the man with our supper? What if it's Duff?"

"Shh!" Nat whispered back. "Stand to the side. If it's not our friend, you run past him first, and I'll—"

He interrupted himself as the footsteps stopped. The latch lifted noisily. Slowly the door squeaked open.

"Boys," a man's friendly voice said, "here's your food. And I've got news. Your boat is heading this way!"

The boys explosively exhaled and eagerly reached into the darkness to feel for the tin of food.

The man added softly, "There's just one problem. A drover name of Duff is bragging around that he knows where you are!"

★　★　★　★　★

The two hounds trotted ahead of Gideon the next morning as he carried the lighted lantern and a milk pail past the hogpen. The boar rushed out of his little shed and ran along the fence, grunting and banging his ugly snout against the lower board rails. "Ah, you don't scare me," Gideon told him, going on toward the barn.

Lantern light from inside showed that the door was opened wide. Fletcher was forking hay down for the mule and cow. "Morning, Gideon. You look mighty perky, so you must have gotten some sleep last night."

"I got some," Gideon replied cheerfully. He hung the lantern on a peg near Fletcher's, picked up the three-legged stool, and moved toward the cow. "How about you?"

"I managed to—" Fletcher broke off as the hounds suddenly charged out of the barn, baying loudly. Their voices blended with hoofbeats of several horses.

Gideon swallowed a huge lump of fear. He said in a low, scared tone, "Here they come!"

"Steady, Gideon!" Fletcher dropped the pitchfork and gripped the boy's shoulders. "Steady!"

Seconds later, Barley Cobb reined in his mule in the open barn door. Several shadowy men on horseback stopped behind him.

Cobb shouted triumphantly, "Fletcher, I done tol' ye that ye'd hang! Gideon, I recken ye'll be swingin' right next to him!"

SO CLOSE, AND
YET...

At first light that morning, Nat and Rufus followed a white abolitionist "conductor" from their hiding place. He led them to the deserted street where they squeezed into a buggy with a carpetbag. Both brothers looked around anxiously, hoping nobody had seen them exit the abandoned tobacco warehouse by the river.

The conductor, an older, thin-faced man with a square chin and sharp blue eyes, drove the horse in silence through dusty streets. Traffic was light, with only a few dray wagons and one carriage in sight.

From under a wide-brimmed hat that hid his curly black hair, Nat glanced down at the white youth's shirt and trousers he wore. "Thanks for bringing these," he said to the driver. "You guessed my size just about right. I look like a planter's son."

The conductor grunted but didn't reply. He had never identified himself. Nat guessed that was to minimize any chance of his "packages" ever being traced back to him.

Darker-skinned Rufus, not having a white father as his older brother did, was dressed in plain clothes to seem to be a body servant to the older youth. Last night when their conductor had brought their food, he also brought them the clothes and the carpetbag. The plan was for Rufus to carry it so they could boldly board the ship without suspicion.

Their conductor had briefly explained that they were to identify themselves to the ship's master with a code word that both boys were sworn never to reveal. He would take them down the

James, then transfer them to a larger vessel for the trip up Chesapeake Bay and a northern state, then on to Canada.

Rufus kept nervously twisting around to look back through the buggy's tiny egg-shaped window, then heaving heavy sighs of relief. Nat repeatedly spoke reassuringly to him on the short drive.

Their vehicle turned off the side street and onto one leading straight to the dock. A small river steamboat had nosed against the long wharf. It was covered with long rows of hogsheads, crates, casks, and bales. Slaves carried some of these across a gangplank onto the vessel.

The driver grunted. "Looks like we're just in time. They're about to cast off."

"Can't be too soon for me!" Rufus declared. He again twisted around to look out the buggy's window. "No!"

Nat instinctively turned to look and saw a horseman turning the corner behind them. He had only seen Duff once, and only briefly, but he knew who it was before his brother breathed a word.

"That's him, and he's following us!"

★   ★   ★   ★   ★

Gideon and Fletcher had remained mute after first asking logical questions of Cobb and the lieutenant of Confederate rangers. The officer stood next to Gideon and Fletcher after announcing that they had reason to suspect a fugitive Yankee soldier was being harbored on the Tugwell property. They had come to search for him.

Gideon licked his dry lips and tried to appear as calm as Fletcher while Cobb joined the investigation. His voice could be heard urging the men to keep looking.

Instead of dwelling on the situation, Gideon tried to occupy his mind by recalling what he knew about the partisans, which was their official designation. As a state organization, they were only a few months old, but following the daring example of the late Ashby Turner, they harassed the Union in whatever way possible.

They did not all dress as Confederates and were not subject to other strict military codes. Property seized from Union forces was divided among the rangers. They were known to make swift attacks on remote outposts, cut communications and supply lines, then temporarily disband to later regroup. Union newspapers and officers raged against these small, effective hit-and-run horsemen.

When the first rays of sunlight poked yellow fingers through the barn's boards and knotholes, Gideon watched the rangers straggle back to the barn empty-handed.

"Sir," a cavalryman in slouch hat and butternut-colored uniform said to the lieutenant, "we have gone through the barn, the smokehouse, harness shed, and a new shed—everywhere a man could hide—with no luck."

Cobb rushed into the barn yelling, "We jist got to keep a-lookin'. He's hereabouts; I know it! Come he'p me look in the fields an' even the swamp!"

Cobb had dressed as a ranger, although he wasn't one. He had a holstered revolver on his hip below a dark blue officer's shell jacket. Gideon suspected it had probably been stolen. Cobb had tied a bright yellow sash around his waist in an effort to look dashing.

"Mr. Cobb," the lieutenant said crisply, removing his brown slouch hat with the left brim turned up. He had stuck a bright red feather in the brim. "I did not believe you when you came to me with this cock-and-bull story." He raised his voice. "Mount up, men."

"No, wait!" Cobb protested, holding up both hands in a futile gesture as the eight rangers moved past him toward their mounts tied outside. "Wait!"

"Cobb!" The lieutenant's voice was hard. "Mr. Fletcher gave his left hand in our noble cause, and you have given me nothing but trouble. But you seemed so certain that I agreed to your request. Yet no one has found a single sign of a fugitive. This search is over."

Gideon wanted to shout with joy but restrained himself.

Fletcher asked politely, "Lieutenant, would you like to search the house? I'm sure this boy's mother would permit that." He looked at Gideon. "Don't you think so?"

"I suppose so. My little brother and sisters must be up by now, what with all the commotion."

"Thank you both," the officer replied, "but I'm sure there's no Yankee hiding in there. Mr. Fletcher, Gideon, I beg your pardon for this unseemly intrusion."

★ ★

He started after his men, but Cobb blocked his way. "Wait! Thar's one place nobody looked: the hog's shed!"

Without thinking, Gideon blurted, "Don't go in there! That's a very mean hog!"

Instantly, all the intruders stopped and looked at him. Gideon gulped, but it was too late.

The officer said quietly, "All right. Two of you men go search there."

"No!" Cobb exclaimed. "Let me!"

The lieutenant turned toward the slave catcher. "Very well. There's no sense in more than one person wading through that smelly pen. We'll watch."

Gideon pleaded, "Please don't—!"

"Lieutenant, listen to him!" Fletcher interrupted.

"I knowed it!" Cobb bellowed in triumph. "I'm right, an' I'm a-gonna prove it!" He ran toward the pigpen.

Gideon closed his eyes and groaned.

★   ★   ★   ★   ★

Emily finished packing her few belongings and walked to the window of her bedchamber. Wistfully, she looked across the tobacco fields to the grove of trees that hid Gideon's house.

From where she sat on the high bed, Julie asked, "Do you think we should go over there or wait here?"

Emily was so deep in thought that the words did not consciously register. Her insides had been twisted into knots all night, wondering if Gideon had been able to carry out the plan they had discussed last evening.

"Well?" Julie prompted.

"What?" Emily asked without turning around.

Julie slid off the bed and walked over to put her arms around Emily's waist. "I know what's on your mind, especially after we heard those horsemen riding by before dawn. I'm going crazy wondering if they found—"

"Don't say it!" Emily said sharply. She took a quick breath before adding, "I'm beside myself wanting to know. But your

★ ★

brother or mother might ask questions if we leave now. We'll just have to wait."

"I suppose so," Julie said, releasing her arms and stepping up beside her cousin.

Together they thoughtfully stared toward Gideon's farm and waited anxiously.

★　★　★　★　★

With his heart pounding in fear, Nat stepped out of the buggy. Out of the corner of his left eye, he could see Duff riding toward the dock, absently flipping a three-foot-long leather whip.

"Careful!" Nat warned his brother in a low tone. "Put the carpetbag back up on your shoulder to keep him from seeing your face. Head for the ship, but walk calmly."

He heard Rufus stifle a sob of fear as he also stepped down, his back to the oncoming rider.

Nat looked up at the driver in the buggy. "I can't thank you enough—" he began.

"No thanks needed," he interrupted. "God be with you both." He clucked to the horse and began to turn around.

The brothers started toward the steamboat. Nat said under his breath, "I see the captain." He whispered to Rufus, "Go across the gangplank and right up to him."

As they neared the vessel, Nat could hear the horse's hooves behind him rapidly getting closer.

★　★　★　★　★

Gideon and Fletcher walked to the barn door, where the lieutenant of the rangers stood with his men. All eyes were on Cobb who jubilantly neared the hogpen.

"Lieutenant," Fletcher said, "I don't want to see any of your men hurt."

"Cobb's not one of us," the officer broke in. "He wants to be, but he's not qualified, even though he took the liberty of dressing up as outlandishly as some of our more dashing cavalrymen do. Like Jeb Stuart and Ashby Turner."

Gideon held his breath as Cobb walked along the outside of

★　★

the pen to where he peered over the top rail.

"Empty!" he called, following the stout rails toward the small shed at the end. "Jist what I thought! A body won't hardly never think o' lookin' in a stinky place like this to hide a Yankee! But I recken all o' ye ain't got as much smarts as me." He reached for the latch high up on the shed door.

"I'm warning you!" Gideon shouted, knowing that the hog was inside the shed, which formed the pen's back end. "Don't open that! You'll let the pig out, and he's mean!"

"I kin take care o' muhse'f," Cobb replied, pulling his pistol with one hand and yanking the door open with the other. "Come outa thar, ye Yankee—"

He didn't finish because the big black hog erupted from the darkened interior with vicious squeals. Cobb started to leap back, but the boar slashed at him with long tusks, ripping one knee-length leather boot in passing. Cobb dropped the gun as the hog stopped, still squealing, pivoted rapidly, and again charged Cobb.

"Look out!" Gideon yelled, unable to help.

Cobb screeched in terror, took two quick steps toward the fence, and leaped upon it. His feet landed about three feet off the ground. The hog slashed hard with wicked tusks, ripping the heel from one boot.

Cobb scrambled like a frightened squirrel toward the top rail. The hog clumsily leaped, his ugly snout missing the slave catcher's feet, but the boar's heavy weight crashed against the fence with a resounding *thud*.

"Ohhhh!" Cobb screamed, teetering on the top rail and wildly flailing his arms to keep his balance. He failed and plopped face-down into the deep muck inside.

The rangers broke into hearty laughter as Cobb sat up sputtering. The hog, realizing he was free, turned and trotted awkwardly across the open yard, into the field, and toward the swamp.

The partisans turned their horses and galloped down the lane, still laughing.

Gideon looked at Fletcher, who grinned at him.

"I can't think of anyone who deserved that more than Cobb,"

★ ★

Fletcher said. "Let's go tell your mother, and then you'd better ride over and see Emily."

"Good idea," Gideon replied. He tried to keep from grinning, but he couldn't stop himself.

★　★　★　★　★

Nat and Rufus boarded the steamer and identified themselves to the ship's master by the secret abolitionist's code word. He was a burly man with fierce red whiskers who gave them a quick, appraising look.

"Welcome aboard. You're my new cabin boy," he said to Rufus. Glancing back at Nat, he added, "You're a new crew member. Now, stand aside until we're under way." He cupped his hands and roared to the crew, "Stand by to raise the gangplank!"

Nearly bursting with joy, the brothers broke into broad smiles and moved toward the rail on the main deck. The last dock worker trotted off the ship, and crewmen sprang to raise the gangplank. For a moment, Nat lost sight of Duff.

A shout from the dock jarred Nat. He saw Duff standing in the stirrups and shouting.

"Captain! Hold up, there! You've got my runaway black boy there by the rail! I'm coming aboard to claim my property!"

★　★　★　★　★

Even though Emily and Julie had every now and then been peering out the windows, it was the geese honking in the lane that alerted the girls that Gideon was coming. They rushed downstairs, past Julie's mother who was sitting in the parlor talking to newly arrived Mrs. Stonum.

The girls slowed to a more ladylike walk as they passed between the Corinthian columns. One displayed the Confederate flag with its seven white stars in a circle.

Emily's mind screamed with eagerness to know what had happened at Gideon's place, but she wanted to get close enough so that no one could overhear.

Gideon reined in beside them and started to slide off the mule's bare back, but Julie didn't wait.

★　★

"What happened?" she asked in a low, excited voice. "Did Brice get away? Did Cobb bring the rangers? We heard them riding by."

"Julie!" Emily chided. "Stop talking so he can answer!"

Gideon took a slow, deep breath before replying.

★ ★ ★ ★ ★

Nat's throat tightened in fear as Duff spurred his horse across the wooden wharf, shouting to the captain to wait. The gangplank crewmen stopped, watching the rider expertly guide his mount through the maze of hogsheads, bales, and crates stacked on the wharf.

Nat felt his younger brother's trembling hand grip his. "He's going to get us!" he cried in a hoarse, scared voice. "He'll nearly whip us to death and then . . ."

Nat didn't hear any more, but he felt the deck begin to vibrate under his feet. The craft pulsated with life and power. In moments, it would be under way, the stern paddle wheel churning down the James River.

Nat knew that under the Fugitive Slave Act of 1850, anyone must surrender a runaway to his master or pay a thousand-dollar fine. Nat realized that if the captain did manage to shove off, his boat would cause him to be identified and he could later be fined. Nat's conscience wouldn't permit him to do that.

"All right, Duff!" he yelled, throwing his hat over the rail. "I'm coming!"

Rufus sputtered, "What . . . what're you—"

"It's the only way!" Nat interrupted, quickly hugging his brother. "You go on! I'll follow someday!"

Releasing his brother, Nat turned to the ship's master. "I'm staying here, so please take care of him! And as soon as I reach the dock, cast off!"

Without waiting for a reply, Nat turned and raced across the deck toward the gangplank while the crew stared in bewilderment.

"Duff!" Nat called when his feet touched the wharf. "I'm coming, but you've got to catch me first!" He dodged behind the nearest stack of barrels and sprinted away.

Duff yelled, raised his whip, spurred his horse, and sent it thundering down the wooden wharf after Nat.

★ ★

THE BATTLE AND
BEYOND

"Cobb showed up with rangers at daybreak, but there was no sign of Brice," Gideon told Emily and Julie.

"Oh, thank God!" Emily exclaimed. "Where was he?"

"Well," Gideon replied, "After we talked last evening, I went back and told my mother and Mr. Fletcher that you had offered to take Brice with you and Mrs. Stonum on your trip north. Then we went to the barn and repeated your idea to Brice. We also told him that Cobb was expected to come with rangers this morning."

Emily asked, "What did Brice say?"

"He said to tell you he appreciated your offer, but that would be unfair to both you and her. She might not go along with the idea, but even if she did, it would put you both in danger if he was caught riding with you."

Emily said softly, "That was a noble thing for him to do."

Gideon wasn't sure he agreed that it was noble, but at least it showed Brice had some redeeming quality. He had done one right thing last night.

"But how did he get away?" Julie asked.

"Well, he said he felt strong enough to ride, and so he insisted on leaving right away. Mama and Mr. Fletcher said we had all done everything we could. Brice would have a chance of finding some of his own troops if he could catch up with Pope's army heading toward Manassas."

"But," Emily protested, "he could also get caught by some of the Confederates going there!"

"We warned him about that," Gideon replied. "He said he'd be careful, but it was a better risk than waiting here for the rangers."

"So he left?" Emily asked.

"Yes, after Mama had made him something to eat on the way and we had given him directions toward Manassas. Well, first he helped remove anything that might show he had been in Mr. Fletcher's quarters for all those days."

Gideon didn't want to admit it, but he felt respect for Brice for cleaning up first instead of immediately riding off. Of course, Gideon and Fletcher had helped, and then afterward they had been too excited to get to sleep for hours.

"So," Gideon said, taking a deep breath, "I hope he makes it back to his own lines."

Emily lightly touched Gideon's arm. "Thank you so much, and thank your mother and Mr. Fletcher. I'm grateful for what all of you did, but I also feel guilty about getting all of you involved in this."

Gideon was relieved to be free of the terrible anxiety that he, his mother, and Fletcher had felt about aiding the enemy. For that, he thought, they would all carry a certain amount of fear or guilt all their lives. He was sure that Emily and Julie felt the same way.

"Now," he said, switching to another concern, "if I could just convince you not to risk going north with all the armies moving between here and the Potomac, I'd feel that this was a very good morning."

Emily sadly shook her head. "I'm sorry, Gideon, but I'm about to burst with stress from worrying about Brice and your family, and knowing I've got to get across the Potomac before those passes expire. I'm leaving early tomorrow."

Gideon had always known this was the plan, but now it was reality. Emily was going away, maybe never to return. That knowledge, combined with the strained night and early morning events, gushed up inside so quickly that he was afraid of losing control of his emotions.

"I'll be back to say good-bye," he said abruptly and leaped upon the mule's bare back. Before either of the girls could say

★ ★

anything more, he turned Hercules and urged him into a trot down the lane. Gideon didn't trust himself to look back.

★　★　★　★　★

Nat dodged among the rows of barrels and bales stacked on the wharf, seeking places too small for Duff to follow on horseback. The white overseers who had been supervising slaves stopped to watch the drama. The dock workers also looked, but none dared interfere or try to help the fleeing youth.

One overseer lunged at Nat, but he leaped over a barrel and evaded him. Nat darted around big hogsheads and bales, fleeing down the wharf away from the steamer. He was quickly short of breath from fear and exertion, but he dared not stop. He glanced back and saw that the horse was delayed in a tight row of crates. But Duff spurred him unmercifully, showing the same determination to catch Nat that had made him hunt Rufus until found.

Duff's shouted threats and snapping of his whip followed Nat as he neared the end of the cargo stacked on the wharf. There, another overseer snatched up a club and moved to intercept Nat. His avenue of escape narrowed. The man waiting with the club was on foot and might be faster than Nat. Nat knew that if he doubled back, he would face Duff.

That left only one other choice: to turn to the right and jump into the river. It was wide and swift, and Nat could not swim.

He slowed, breathing hard, frantically trying to make a decision. The man with the club was running toward him. Duff was gaining on him from behind. The steamboat's deep bass whistle warned that the vessel was getting under way. Nat took a quick look toward it. His brother stood at the rail, arms outstretched, mouth open as though crying out, but Nat could not hear him over the sound of the reversed paddle wheels churning the water.

Nat waved to his brother, fought back a sudden rush of hot tears, and stopped, waiting for Duff. In seconds, he leaped upon Nat, bearing him to the splintery wharf. Duff snarled like an animal, shouting obscenities and viciously pummelling Nat with a hard fist while striking with the whip in the other hand.

Nat did not cry out but escaped into his mind, not feeling the

★　★

pain so much. Duff would return him to Briarstone for the reward. William would severely whip him before probably selling him down the river into the Deep South, where escape was almost impossible.

Through eyes dimmed by pain and tears, Nat had a last glimpse of the steamer moving toward midstream. Rufus no longer stood at the rail, for the master had moved between him and the dock.

As Duff's beating slowed, Nat was strangely content. Rufus was safely on his way to freedom. Nat had escaped before. He could do it again because his mother was right: Winning was in the mind and not the muscles.

His mother, sister, and now one brother were on the long road to freedom. Somehow Nat would find a way to continue searching for his remaining two brothers. Then someday, they would all be free.

★ ★ ★ ★ ★

Shortly after daybreak the next day, Gideon stood outside the glistening white pillars at Briarstone while Emily said good-bye to everyone. Gideon felt like an outsider as he watched and listened.

A four-wheeled town coach with the black body, distinctive gold stripe, and Briarstone Plantation crest was parked near the front door. A pair of matched bay horses waited in the carriage's red shafts.

Toombs, the white overseer, stood with his hat in one hand and his horse's reins in the other. "Miss Emily," he said with a slight bow, "if you ever return, you're welcome to ride with me anytime."

Her reply was so soft that Gideon didn't hear it, but he caught William's final words: "Mother and I deeply appreciate what you did while I was laid up."

"Thank you," she replied. "I thank you for making my stay pleasant. I hope you'll tell your mother the same when she's feeling better."

"We're sorry you're leaving," William said. "If you ever want

★ ★

to come back, this is your home, too."

That surprised Gideon, who saw from Emily's expression that she was also astonished. She murmured her thanks, then turned to hug Julie.

She softly pleaded, "Please don't go, Emily. It's not safe! If those armies—"

"Please don't make this harder than it already is," Emily broke in. "I know it's dangerous, and so does Mrs. Stonum. But she's willing to risk the trip, and our passes will expire if we don't go while we can. When Uncle George returns with the carriage, you'll know we got through to the Potomac safely."

"Just the same," Julie protested, tears in her eyes and a quiver in her voice, "I had to ask one more time, just as the Toombs children did last night. They want you to stay and help teach them. Even William said it would be all right if you stay."

"It's been very pleasant," Emily replied. "But my heart longs to be back in Illinois. . . ." Her voice broke and she turned away, but not before Gideon saw tears on her eyelashes.

Julie put her arms around Emily's shoulders and held her close, but neither spoke while Gideon waited for his turn to say good-bye.

He suffered from a sad, empty feeling. Once before, he had said good-bye to Emily when she left for Richmond, but it hadn't hurt like this. He was almost a year older now and was keenly aware of how much he didn't want her to leave. Yet he could not bring himself to say that.

Riding over on Hercules, Gideon had tried to think what he should say as he neared the house, which stood solid and square at the end of the lane of poplars.

William had greeted him cordially, seeming to have forgotten his cold remarks when Gideon came for his first lesson with Emily. Gideon wasn't sure he really trusted William's apparent change of heart, but it was nice to not be treated like white trash for a change.

With a dainty sniff, Emily released Julie and turned to Gideon. Teardrops on her violet eyes shimmered like morning dew on roses.

"Gideon," she said in a low, soft tone, "I don't know how I can ever tell you how much . . ." She stopped, biting her lower lip.

"I can't tell you, either," he said quietly. "But someday I hope to write what I'm thinking, and I hope you'll read it and know."

"I'll watch for your name in the papers, and one day, in a book. I'll be proud to say, 'I know him.' "

Gideon's emotions burst uncontrollably, making him turn away so she could not see his own eyes suddenly fill with tears. Embarrassed, he leaped upon Hercules' broad back and rode away, hating himself for breaking down and wishing he had said good-bye properly.

It was only when he reached the end of the lane where she could not see his eyes clearly that he turned around. She stood where he had left her. Slowly, she lifted her right hand in a fare-well gesture.

He waved back. "Good-bye, Emily," he whispered.

★ ★ ★ ★ ★

The broad Potomac River curved south and west in the shape of a modified fishhook, but the bridge Emily needed to cross was farther north. At dawn of the second morning after leaving Briar-stone in the carriage with Mrs. Stonum, there was the distant thunder of cannon. Soon afterward, Emily watched through the window as black columns of smoke rose ominously from toward Manassas.

She was fearful of what that meant when she heard a sharp order to halt, and George stopped the vehicle.

Mrs. Stonum said, "It's probably a picket." She stuck her head out the window. "Yes, a couple of them."

Emily leaned out the window on the other side. An armed but barefoot Confederate soldier, dressed in a ragged gray uniform and slouch hat with a bayonet fixed on his rifle, watched the driver. An infantryman in tattered butternut uniform approached Mrs. Stonum's side of the vehicle.

She asked him, "What's the matter?"

The infantryman bent to quickly scan the interior before answering. "Big battle started today. Sorry to tell you ladies, but you've got to turn back."

"Turn back?" Emily exclaimed, leaning forward to look at the young soldier's face from under her bonnet. "We can't! We've got to get across the Potomac before our passes expire!"

He stuck his head inside the carriage to get a better look at her. A smile touched his beardless face. "Miss, I ain't seen a purty gal since I left home, and I ain't never seen one as downright purty as you. But I got my orders. You and your mother have to turn back."

"But why?" Emily protested, not bothering to explain that they were not mother and daughter. "That smoke is way off—"

"It's closer than you think," he interrupted. "And the battle's coming this way. We heard that Manassas is burned up. General Lee, Jackson, and some others attacked several Union generals, including McClellan and Pope. The fighting's getting hotter, and no telling when it'll be over. Sorry, but my orders are that nobody passes here."

"Then we'll go around," Emily exclaimed. "We've only got five days to get across the river!"

"Miss," he said sharply, "you don't understand! The roads in all directions are filled with troops trying to get to the battlefield. When it's over, dead and wounded men will be scattered everywhere, not to mention horses and equipment. It's going to be awful!"

Emily involuntarily drew back, causing him to soften his tone. "Miss, we hear tell that there's upwards of a hundred thousand Yankees spread out north of here. We ain't got near that many, but this here is our own land. We don't aim to let them take it from us. Now, please, turn around and go back."

Mrs. Stonum said to him, "Please give us a moment."

As he nodded and stepped away, Emily cried, "I don't want to turn back! It took almost a year for me to get our passes, and I might never get another one! Everything that's important to me is in Illinois."

The words poured out, faster and faster. "I want to see my friend Jessie and the place where I grew up. I want to visit the

★ ★

graves of my parents and my brothers. I want to go *home*, not turn back!"

The widow gently touched the girl's anguished face. "We don't always get to do what we want. Remember, God's thoughts and ways are higher than ours. Maybe there's a higher reason why you've been unable to leave the South."

Emily recalled Joseph's unwanted sojourn in Egypt and how that turned out for good. She remembered Gideon suggesting that maybe God's place for her was here, not in Illinois. *But that's not what I want!*

In agony of spirit, Emily took the precious pass from her bag and studied the expiration date. Slowly, her eyes moved to the top of the coach, where George sat on the outside seat. Sighing, Emily turned to Mrs. Stonum.

"I'm willing to try going around," Emily said, "but I can't risk your life, or George's. Let's turn back."

★   ★   ★   ★   ★

At dawn on Monday, September 1, Gideon headed for the barn, anguishing because there had been no word from Emily since she and Mrs. Stonum left. That was bad.

In the village yesterday after church, there had been telegraphic reports about a great Confederate victory at Manassas. Some Federal generals, including McClellan and Pope, had been badly defeated. Pope was expected to lose his command and be relocated far away from Virginia.

Robert E. Lee's and "Stonewall" Jackson's attacks against superior Union forces had again put Lee's victorious armies within striking distance of Washington. If rumors were true that Lee was preparing to invade the North, Confederates might end the war by seizing the Union capital only about twenty-five miles away.

Gideon entered the barn and greeted Fletcher where he was currying the mule. "I've been thinking," Gideon began, "your friends and neighbors won't need help in the Shenandoah Valley since Pope's been driven out. So you won't have to leave here after the harvest."

Fletcher stopped currying the mule. "I've been considering

★   ★

talking to your mother about that."

"Really?" Gideon's excitement soared. "Why don't you go do that right now? I'll finish the chores here."

Fletcher's mouth showed the faintest hint of a smile. "Maybe after breakfast, and after I go look for that runaway hog again."

"I'll do that," Gideon quickly volunteered. "You stay and talk to Mama."

Fletcher nodded thoughtfully. "Maybe I will."

★ ★ ★ ★ ★

Right after they'd eaten, Gideon mounted Hercules, whistled to the dogs, and headed toward the public road where Fletcher had reported seeing fresh hog tracks. Gideon hoped that Fletcher would stay on, but that did not ease Gideon's worry about Emily. He spotted the hog's tracks in the road's deep dust just as the hounds suddenly bawled and ran ahead.

Gideon looked up to see a carriage approaching. He stared in uncertainty before a blond head popped out of the window.

"Emily!" he shouted, waving and drumming his heels against the mule's flanks. "Emily! You're back!"

She smiled broadly and waved her bonnet as Gideon forced Hercules into a trot.

Behind him, from the house, for the first time in many months, Gideon heard his mother begin to sing.

EPILOGUE

October 14, 1933

The Confederate victory at Second Manassas (or Bull Run, as the Yankees call it) gave hope to the South. For the first time, the way was open for General Lee to carry the war back to those who had invaded the South. It was a historic time, but my interest was more on Emily, Nat, and the others who were then part of my growing-up years.

Emily told me that she and Mrs. Stonum had been delayed getting back because main roads were blocked by troops, wagons, and equipment moving to the battle.

She had wept in disappointment that her own personal goal had again been thwarted, but she realized that war required individuals to sacrifice their personal desires for the good of others.

Her aunt and William commended her for compassion in helping them at what turned out to be a great personal sacrifice to herself. She still hoped to someday return to Illinois, but for the present, she resolutely faced whatever awaited her at Briarstone.

Nat learned that the haunting bugle call he had first heard along the Potomac was known as "Taps." He said that he would never forget Rufus at the steamboat's rail with arms outstretched and mouth open as though crying out to him. Nat's love and loyalty made him willing to return to bondage so that his brother might go free.

Nat and Rufus were among some four million slaves held in eleven Southern states when the war began. Only a small percentage of them ever escaped, but some of those who did so took the road to freedom more than once. As for me, these many years later, I still have pangs of guilt about aiding a Yankee enemy who had invaded Virginia's sacred soil. But I believed with my mother and Fletcher that helping anybody in need is right. None of us ever revealed our secret, which I haven't disclosed until now. The choices we made determined our destinies, but no one can now be hurt except me. Let history judge our motives and actions.

As I write this page, my thoughts leap back to what happened to Emily, Nat, and me after September 1862, when General Lee invaded the North. I'll relive those dramatic days when I again open my boyhood journal.